Horace Elisha Scudder

Fables and Folk Stories

Horace Elisha Scudder

Fables and Folk Stories

ISBN/EAN: 9783744778640

Printed in Europe, USA, Canada, Australia, Japan

Cover: Foto ©Andreas Hilbeck / pixelio.de

More available books at **www.hansebooks.com**

The Riverside Literature Series

FABLES AND FOLK STORIES

BY

HORACE E. SCUDDER

HOUGHTON, MIFFLIN AND COMPANY
Boston: 4 Park Street; New York: 85 Fifth Avenue
Chicago: 378-388 Wabash Avenue
The Riverside Press, Cambridge

The Riverside Press, Cambridge, Mass., U. S. A.
Electrotyped and Printed by H. O. Houghton & Company.

PREFACE.

As soon as a child has learned to make out simple sentences, the wise teacher looks about for something which it is worth while to read. The primer and the reader are necessarily simple, but the simplicity is, for the most part, below the child's intelligence. Children can understand by hearing long before they can understand by reading ; during the period when they are mastering the several combinations in which a boy, a rat, and a cat can be placed, and are acquiring the power of reading at sight, they are listening to books which are by no means so barren in their simplicity, and as soon as they are able to read the little stories which they find in their first readers they leave them behind.

It is interesting to note, however, that there are certain parts of their primer which they never leave behind and never forget. The

Mother Goose Melodies and the proverbs which
form some of the early sentences taught them,
the quaint nursery tales like The Story of Chicken
Licken, The Old Woman and Her Pig, The
Three Bears, — these they remember and separate from the chaff of the ordinary reading exer-
cises by the winnowing fan of their spiritual
judgment. They perceive, even thus early, what
is literature and what is not literature; they
hold to that, and discard this.

Literature, for the sake of which the art of
reading is acquired, is never left behind, and it
becomes of importance to give children, as soon
as may be, enduring forms on which they may
exercise their newly acquired power, and in
which they may take the first draughts of a
pleasure as genuine as any to be enjoyed when
they come into the full possession of their blos-
soming faculty of imagination.

There are two forms of literary art which belong rightfully to the early period of childhood:
the Fable and the Folk-Story. The fable is
oriental, and it is antique. It is also exceed-
ingly current and universal as a coin of speech.
The man and the boy both use it, and while in
its full form it seems most capable of giving

pleasure to the child, its conventionalism enables the mature mind to accept it without any sense of condescension to childish things. It is the most perfect literary instrument of association between the young and the old, and becomes therefore by right the first possession of children in literature.

There are good reasons, from its structure, why the fable should be adapted to the use of children. In the first place, it is short; the child has the pleasure of reading an entire story at one sitting. Then it is of animals, and animals are the natural companions of the child. Again, it is interesting and novel; it appeals to his imagination, for it represents the animal as having human properties; and it suggests a plain moral. It is true, the morality of the fable usually is a prudential one, but prudence is a virtue which comes early in the lessons of life. We may rest with confidence in the worth of stories which have been tested by generations and centuries of use.

The child, therefore, who reads the classic fables has begun his acquaintance with permanent literature. He is reading what the world has chosen to remember. He is applying his new powers to that which is worth while. He is beginning to receive the impressions which literature has made upon human life, and the early impressions which he thus receives will never become even consciously faint. That is to say, there never will come a time in his life when the fable may not still give him pleasure ; but the time already has come when the reading-book which he read last week no longer can excite his interest or hold his attention. Every one will recognize the important step which a child has taken when he has entered the current of the world's lasting literature.

The folk-story is more exclusively the child's, and is shared by older people rather through memory and association than by continued use. Every people of Europe, and the Americans by composite inheritance, have a body of household tales which, whatever their antiquity, have become the peculiar possession of Christendom. Scholars have made comparative studies of these tales, but they have based such studies upon the stories as they have been transmitted, not so much through books as through recital, from mother to child, in the course of generations. While poets were forming the literature which fills our libraries, the unlettered people were repeating to each other these familiar, poetic tales. Now and then some romancer would take one of them and set it forth in finer, more fantastic garb, but for the most part the form was a homely one, which did not vary greatly from one age to another.

In preparing this book for use in schools, I have drawn upon two volumes I had already published, *The Book of Fables* and *The Book of Folk-Stories*, and have added others not there given. In writing out the fables, so far as they were from Æsop, I have endeavored to preserve the exact lines of the original story, and to use phrases which present no extraordinary difficulties to a child. It has not been my purpose to turn these fables into words of one syllable, for such words and the construction which they compel often produce an artificial effect, of greater difficulty to the young reader than the more natural arrangement of words which may happen to have two syllables or even three.

In the case of the folk-stories, I have not departed knowingly from the generally accepted structure. I have tried simply to use words and constructions which present the fewest difficul-

ties. I should like to believe that I have suc-
ceeded to some extent in thinking out these
stories as a child would think them, and so have
used that order and choice of words which would
be the natural expression of a child's mind. By
a mingling of the two forms, greater variety has
been secured, and the arrangement has regard
to the order of ease in reading.

H. E. SCUDDER.

CAMBRIDGE, MASS., *August* 13, 1890.

CONTENTS

FABLES AND FOLK STORIES.

LITTLE ONE EYE, LITTLE TWO EYES, AND LITTLE THREE EYES.

I.

THE GOAT.

THERE was once a woman who had three daughters. The eldest was called Little One Eye, because she had only one eye in the middle of her forehead. The second was called Little Two Eyes, because she had two eyes like other people. The youngest was called Little Three Eyes, because she had three eyes; the third eye was also in the middle of her forehead.

Because Little Two Eyes looked like other people, her sisters and her mother could not bear her. They said: —

" You have two eyes and are no better than anybody else. You do not belong to us." They knocked her about, and gave her shabby clothes, and fed her with food left over from their meals; in short, they vexed her whenever they could.

One day Little Two Eyes was sent into the fields to look after the goat. She was quite hungry, because her sisters had given her so little to eat, and she sat down and began to cry. She cried so hard that a little stream of tears ran out of each eye. All at once a wise woman stood near her, and asked : —

"Little Two Eyes, why do you cry ? " Little Two Eyes said : —

"Have I not need to cry ? Because I have two eyes, like other people, my sisters and my mother cannot bear me. They knock me about; they give me shabby clothes; and they feed me only with the food left over from their table. To-day they have given me so little that I am quite hungry." The wise woman said : —

"Little Two Eyes, dry your eyes, and I will tell you what to do. Only say to your goat: 'Little goat, bleat ; little table, rise,' and a neatly-laid table will stand before you, covered with food. Eat as much as you like. When you have had all you want, only say : 'Little goat, bleat ; little table, away,' and it will be gone." Then the wise woman disappeared. Little Two Eyes thought : —

"I must try at once, for I am much too hungry to wait." So she said : —

"Little goat, bleat ; little table, rise." In a

twinkling there stood before her a little table covered with a white cloth. On it were laid a plate, knife and fork, and silver spoon. The nicest food was on the plate, smoking hot. Then Little Two Eyes began to eat, and found the food very good. When she had had enough, she said : —

"Little goat, bleat; little table, away." In an instant the table was gone.

" That is a fine way to keep house," thought Little Two Eyes, and she was quite merry.

At the end of the day Little Two Eyes drove her goat home. She found a dish with some food in it; her sisters had put it aside for her from their table, but she did not taste it. She did not need it.

The next day she went out again with her goat, and did not take the few crusts which her sisters put aside for her. This went on for several days. At last her sisters said to each other : —

" All is not right with Little Two Eyes. She always leaves her food; she used to eat all that was given her; she must have found some other way to be fed."

They meant to find out what Little Two Eyes did. So the next time that Little Two Eyes set out, Little One Eye came to her and said : —

"I will go with you into the field, and see that the goat is well taken care of, and feeds in the best pasture." But Little Two Eyes saw what Little One Eye had in her mind. So she drove the goat into the long grass, and said : —

"Come, Little One Eye, we will sit down and I will sing to you." Little One Eye sat down; she was tired after her long walk in the hot sun, and Little Two Eyes began to sing : —

"Are you awake, Little One Eye? Are you asleep, Little One Eye? Are you awake, Little One Eye? Are you asleep, Little One Eye? Are you awake? Are you asleep? Awake? Asleep?" By this time Little One Eye had shut her one eye and was fast asleep. When Little Two Eyes saw this, she said softly : —

"Little goat, bleat; little table, rise;" and she sat at the table and ate and drank till she had had enough. Then she said as before : —

"Little goat, bleat; little table, away," and in a twinkling all was gone.

Little Two Eyes now awoke Little One Eye, and said : —

"Little One Eye, why do you not watch? You have been asleep, and the goat could have run all over the world. Come! let us go home." So home they went, and Little Two Eyes again did not touch the dish. The others asked Little One Eye what Little Two Eyes did in the field. But she could only say : —

"Oh, I fell asleep out there."

II.

THE TREE.

THE next day, the mother said to Little Three Eyes : —

"This time you must go with Little Two Eyes, and see if any one brings her food and drink." Then Little Three Eyes said to Little Two ,Eyes : —

"I will go with you into the field, and see that the goat is well taken care of, and feeds in the best pasture." But Little Two Eyes saw what Little Three Eyes had in her mind. So she drove the goat into the long grass, and said : —

"Come, Little Three Eyes, we will sit down, and I will sing to you." Little Three Eyes sat down; she was tired after her long walk in the hot sun, and Little Two Eyes began to sing, as before : —

"Are you awake, Little Three Eyes?" but instead of going on, —

"Are you asleep, Little Three Eyes?" she did not think, and sang : —

"Are you asleep, Little Two Eyes?" and went on : —

"Are you awake, Little Three Eyes? Are you asleep, Little Two Eyes? Are you awake? Are you asleep? Awake? Asleep?" By this time the two eyes of Little Three Eyes fell asleep, but the third eye did not go to sleep, for it was not spoken to by the verse. Little Three Eyes, to be sure, shut it, and made believe that it went to sleep. Then she opened it a little way and watched Little Two Eyes.

When Little Two Eyes thought Little Three Eyes was fast asleep, she said softly : —

"Little goat, bleat; little table, rise;" and she sat at ·the table and ate and drank till she had had enough. Then she said as before : —

"Little goat, bleat ; little table, away." But Little Three Eyes had seen everything. Little Two Eyes now woke Little Three Eyes, and said : —

"Little Three Eyes, why do you not watch? You have been asleep, and the goat could have run all over the world. Come ! let us go home." So home they went, and Little Two Eyes again did not touch the dish. Then Little Three Eyes said to the mother : —

"I know why the proud thing does not eat. She says to the goat: 'Little goat, bleat; little table, rise,' and there stands a table before her. It is covered with the very best of things to eat, much better than anything we have. When she has had enough to eat, she says: 'Little goat, bleat; little table, away,' and all is gone. I have seen it just as it is. She put two of my eyes to sleep with a song, but the one in my forehead stayed awake." Then the mother cried out : —

"Shall she be better off than we are?" With that she took a knife and killed the goat. Poor Little Two Eyes went to the field, and sat down and began to cry. All at once the wise woman stood near her, and asked : —

"Little Two Eyes, why do you cry?" Little Two Eyes said : —

"Have I not need to cry? My mother has killed the goat. Now I must suffer hunger and thirst again." The wise woman said : —

"Little Two Eyes, dry your eyes, and I will tell you what to do. Beg your sisters to give you the heart of the goat. Then bury it in the ground before the door of the house. All will go well with you." Then the wise woman was gone, and Little Two Eyes went home and said to her sisters : —

"Sisters, give me some part of my goat.

I do not ask for anything but the heart."
They laughed, and said : —

"You can have that, if you do not want
anything else." Little Two Eyes took the heart
and buried it in the ground before the door
of the house.

Next morning the sisters woke and saw a
splendid tree in front of the house. It had
leaves of silver and fruit of gold. It was wonderful to behold; and they could not think
how the tree had come there in the night.
Only Little Two Eyes saw that the tree had
grown out of the heart of the goat. Then the
mother said to Little One Eye : —

"Climb up, my child, and pluck some fruit
from the tree." Little One Eye climbed the
tree. She put out her hand to take a golden
apple, but the branch sprang back. This took
place every time. Try as hard as she could,
she could not get a single apple. Then the
mother said : —

"Little Three Eyes, do you climb up. You
can see better with your three eyes than Little One Eye can." Down came Little One Eye,
and Little Three Eyes climbed the tree. But
it was with her just as it had been with Little One Eye. She put out her hand, and the
branch sprang back. At last the mother tried,
but it was the same with her. She could not

get a single apple.   Then Little Two Eyes
said : —

"Let me try."

"You!" they all cried. "You, with your
two eyes like other people! What can you
do?" But Little Two Eyes climbed the tree,
and the branch did not spring back. The
golden apples dropped into her hands, and she
brought down her apron full of them. Her
mother took them away from her, and her two
sisters were angry because they had failed, and
they were more cruel than ever to Little Two
Eyes.

III.

THE PRINCE.

WHILE they stood by the tree, the Prince
came riding near on a fine horse.

"Quick, Little Two Eyes," said her sisters,
"creep under this cask; we are ashamed of
you;" and they threw an empty cask over her,
and pushed the golden apples under it. The
Prince rode up and gazed at the splendid tree.
"Is this splendid tree yours?" he asked of
the sisters. "If you will give me a branch
from it, I will give you anything you wish."
Then Little One Eye and Little Three Eyes
said the tree was theirs, and they would break

off a branch for him. They put out their hands, but again the branches sprang back. Then the Prince said : —

"This is very strange. The tree is yours, and yet you cannot pluck the fruit."

They kept on saying that the tree was theirs, but while they were saying this, Little Two Eyes rolled a few of the apples out from under the cask. The Prince saw them, and asked : —

"Why! where did these golden apples come from? Who is under the cask?" Little One Eye and Little Three Eyes told the Prince that they had a sister.

"But she does not show herself," they said. "She is just like other people. She has two eyes." Then the Prince called : —

"Little Two Eyes! come out!" So Little Two Eyes was very glad and crept out from under the cask.

"Can you get me a branch from the tree?"

"Yes," said Little Two Eyes, "I can, for the tree is mine." Then she climbed the tree and broke off a branch. It had silver leaves and golden fruit, and she gave it to the Prince. Then the Prince said : —

"Little Two Eyes, what shall I give you for it?"

"Oh," said Little Two Eyes, "I suffer hunger

and thirst all day long. If you would take me with you, I should be happy."

So the Prince lifted Little Two Eyes upon his horse, and they rode away. He took her to his father's house and made her Princess, and she had plenty to eat and drink, and good clothes to wear. Best of all, the Prince loved her, and she had no more hard knocks and cross words.

Now, when Little Two Eyes rode away with the Prince, the sisters said : —

" Well, we shall have the tree. We may not pluck the fruit, but every one will stop to see it and come to us and praise it." The next morning they went to look at the tree, and it was gone.

Little Two Eyes lived long and happily. One day, two poor women came to her, and asked for something to eat. Little Two Eyes looked at their faces and knew them. They were Little One Eye and Little Three Eyes. They were so poor that they were begging bread from door to door. Little Two Eyes brought them into the house and was very good to them. Then they both were sorry for the evil they had once done their sister.

THE CRAB AND HIS MOTHER.

SAID his Mother to a Crab : " Why do you walk so crooked, child ? Walk straight."

" Mother," said he, " show me the way, and I will try to walk like you." But as long as she could not walk straight, her son laughed at her advice.

THE BOYS AND THE FROGS.

A COMPANY of idle Boys were watching some Frogs by the side of a pond, and as fast as any of the Frogs lifted their heads the Boys would pelt them down again with stones.

" Boys," said one of the Frogs, " you forget that, though this may be fun for you, it is death to us."

THE WIND AND THE SUN.

THE Wind and the Sun had a dispute as to which of the two was the stronger; they agreed that the one should be called stronger who should first make a man in the road take off his cloak.

The Wind began to blow great guns, but the man only drew his cloak closer about him to keep out the cold. At last the gust was over.

Then the Sun took his turn. He shone, and it was warm and bright. The man opened his cloak, threw it back, and at last took it off, and lay down in the shade where it was cool.

So the Sun carried his point against the Wind.

This fable teaches that it is often easier to persuade men than it is to force them.

LITTLE RED-RIDING-HOOD.

ONCE upon a time there lived in a certain village a little girl. Her mother was very fond of her, and her grandmother doted on her even more. This good old woman made for her a red cloak, which suited the child so well that ever after she was called Little Red-Riding-Hood.

One day her mother made some cakes, and said to Little Red-Riding-Hood : —

"Go, my dear, and see how grandmother does, for I hear that she has been very ill. Carry her a cake and a little pot of butter."

Little Red-Riding-Hood set out at once to go to her grandmother, who lived in another village. As she was going through the wood she met a large Wolf. He had a very great mind to eat her up; but he dared not, for there were some wood-choppers near by. So he asked her : —

"Where are you going, little girl?" The poor child did not know that it was dangerous to stop and talk with the Wolf, and she said : —

"I am going to see my grandmother, and carry her a cake and a little pot of butter from my mother."

"Does she live far off?" asked the Wolf.

"Oh, yes. It is beyond that mill you see there, at the first house in the village."

"Well," said the Wolf, "I will go and see her, too. I will go this way; do you go that, and we will see who will be there soonest."

At this the Wolf began to run as fast as he could, taking the nearest way, and Little Red-Riding-Hood went by the farthest. She stopped often to chase a butterfly, or pluck a flower, and so she was a good while on the way. The Wolf was soon at the old woman's house, and knocked at the door — tap, tap!

"Who is there?"

"Your grandchild, Little Red-Riding-Hood," replied the Wolf, changing his voice. "I have brought you a cake and a pot of butter from mother." The good grandmother, who was ill in bed, called out : —

"Pull the string, and the latch will go up."

The Wolf pulled the string, and the latch went up. The door opened, and he jumped in, and fell upon the old woman, and ate her up in less than no time, for he had not tasted food for three days. He then shut the door, and got into the grandmother's bed. By and by, Little Red-

Riding-Hood came and knocked at the door — tap, tap!

"Who is there?"

Little Red-Riding-Hood heard the big voice of the Wolf, and at first she was afraid. Then she thought her grandmother must have a bad cold, and be very hoarse, so she answered: —

"Little Red-Riding-Hood. I have brought you a cake and a pot of butter from mother." The Wolf softened his voice as much as he could, and called out: —

"Pull the string, and the latch will go up."

Little Red-Riding-Hood pulled the string, and the latch went up, and the door opened. The Wolf was hiding under the bed clothes and called out in a muffled voice: —

"Put the cake and the pot of butter on the shelf, and come to bed."

Little Red-Riding-Hood made ready for bed. Then she looked with wonder at her grandmother, who had changed so much, and she said: —

"Grandmother, what great arms you have!"

"The better to hug you, my dear."

"Grandmother, what great ears you have!"

"The better to hear you, my dear."

"Grandmother, what great eyes you have!"

"The better to see you, my dear."

"Grandmother, what great teeth you have!"

" The better to eat you." And at this the wicked Wolf sprang up and fell upon poor Little Red-Riding-Hood and ate her all up.

THE CROW AND THE PITCHER.

A Crow that was very thirsty found a Pitcher with a little water in it, but the water lay so low that she could not come at it.

She tried first to break the Pitcher, and then to overturn it, but it was both too strong and too heavy for her. She thought at last of a way, for she dropped a great many little pebbles into the Pitcher, and thus raised the water until she could reach it.

A COUNTRY FELLOW AND THE RIVER.

A stupid Boy, who was sent to market by the good old woman, his Mother, to sell butter and cheese, made a stop by the way at a swift river, and laid himself down on the bank there, until it should run out.

About midnight, home he goes to his Mother, with all his market goods back again.

" Why, how now, my Son ?" says she. " What have we here ? "

" Why, Mother, yonder is a river that has been running all this day, and I stayed till just now, waiting for it to run out; and there it is, running still."

"My Son," says the good woman, "thy head and mine will be laid in the grave many a day before this river has all run by. You will never sell your butter and cheese if you wait for that."

THE ELVES AND THE SHOEMAKER.

THERE was once a Shoemaker who worked very hard and was honest. Still, he could not earn enough to live on, and at last all he had in the world was gone except just leather enough to make one pair of shoes. He cut these out at night, and meant to rise early the next morning to make them up.

His heart was light amid all his troubles, for his conscience was clear. So he went quietly to bed, left all his cares to God, and fell asleep. In the morning he said his prayers and sat down to work, when, to his great wonder, there stood the shoes, already made, upon the table.

The good man knew not what to say or think. He looked at the work; there was not one false stitch in the whole job; all was neat and true.

That same day a customer came in, and the shoes pleased him so well that he readily paid a price higher than usual for them. The Shoemaker took the money and bought leather enough to make two pairs more. He cut out the work in the evening and went to bed early. He wished to be up with the sun and get to work.

He was saved all trouble, for when he got up in the morning, the work was done, ready to his hand. Pretty soon buyers came in, who paid him well for his goods. So he bought leather enough for four pairs more.

He cut out the work again over night, and found it finished in the morning as before. So it went on for some time. What was got ready at night was always done by daybreak, and the good man soon was well to do.

One evening, at Christmas time, he and his wife sat over the fire, chatting, and he said : —

" I should like to sit up and watch to-night, that we may see who it is that comes and does my work for me." His wife liked the thought. So they left the light burning, and hid themselves behind a curtain to see what would happen.

As soon as it was midnight there came two little Elves. They sat upon the Shoemaker's bench, took up all the work that was cut out, and began to ply their little fingers. They stitched and rapped and tapped at such a rate that the Shoemaker was all amazement, and could not take his eyes off them for a moment.

On they went busily till the job was quite done, and the shoes stood, ready for use, upon the table. This was long before daybreak. Then they bustled away as quick as lightning. The next day the wife said to the Shoemaker : —

" These little Elves have made us rich, and we ought to be thankful to them and do them some good in return. I am quite vexed to see them run about as they do. They have nothing upon their backs to keep off the cold. I 'll tell you what we must do ; I will make each of them a shirt, and a coat and waistcoat, and a pair of pantaloons into the bargain. Do you make each of them a little pair of shoes."

The good Shoemaker liked the thought very well. One evening, he and his wife had the clothes ready, and laid them on the table instead of the work they used to cut out. Then they went and hid behind the curtain to watch what the little Elves would do.

At midnight the Elves came in and were going to sit down at their work as usual; but when they saw the clothes lying there for them, they laughed and were in high glee. They dressed themselves in the twinkling of an eye, and danced and capered and sprang about as merry as could be, till at last they danced out of the door, and over the green.

The Shoemaker saw them no more, but everything went well with him from that time forward as long as he lived.

THE ASS IN THE LION'S SKIN.

THE Ass once dressed himself in the Lion's skin, and went about scaring all the little beasts. He met the Fox, and tried to scare him too, but the Fox stopped, and said : —

"Well, to be sure, I should have been scared like the others, if I had not heard you bray and seen your ears stick out."

THE STAR–GAZER.

A CERTAIN wise man was wont to go out every evening and gaze at the stars. Once his walk took him outside of the town, and as he was looking with all his eyes into the sky, and did not see where he was going, he fell into a ditch.

He was in a sad plight, and set up a cry. A man who was passing by heard him, and stopped to see what was the matter.

"Ah, sir," said he, "when you are trying to make out what is in the sky, you do not see what is on the earth."

THE BOY AND THE NETTLE.

A Boy playing in the fields was stung by a Nettle. He ran home to his Mother, and told her that he had but touched the weed, and it had stung him.

"It was just touching it that stung you," said she. "The next time you meddle with a Nettle, grasp it boldly, and it will not hurt you."

THE DOG IN THE MANGER.

A Dog once made his bed in a manger. He could not eat the grain there, and he would not let the Ox eat it, who could.

THE BOY WHO STOLE APPLES.

An Old Man found a rude Boy up in one of his trees, stealing apples, and bade him come down. The young rogue told him plainly that he would not.

"Won't you?" said the Old Man. "Then I will fetch you down." So he pulled up some tufts of grass and threw them at him; but this only made the youngster laugh.

"Well, well," said the Old Man. If neither words nor grass will do, I will try what virtue there is in stones." With that he pelted the

Boy heartily with stones, which soon made him clamber down from the tree and beg the Old Man's pardon.

HANS IN LUCK.

I.

THE SILVER, THE HORSE, THE COW, AND THE PIG.

HANS had served his master seven years, and at last said to him : —

" Master, my time is up; I should like to go home and see my mother; so give me my wages." And the Master said : —

" You have been a good and faithful servant, so your pay shall be handsome." Then he gave him a piece of silver as big as his head.

Hans took out his handkerchief, put the piece of silver into it, hung it over his shoulder, and jogged off homeward. As he went lazily on, dragging one foot after the other, a man came in sight, trotting along gayly on a capital horse.

" Ah!" said Hans aloud, " what a fine thing it is to ride on horseback! there he sits as if he were at home in his chair; he trips against no stones, spares his shoes, and gets on he hardly knows how." The Horseman heard this, and said : —

"Well, Hans, why do you go on foot then?"

"Ah," said he, "I have this load to carry; to be sure it is silver, but it is so heavy that I cannot hold up my head, and it hurts my shoulder sadly."

"What do you say to changing?" asked the Horseman. "I will give you my horse, and you shall give me your silver."

"With all my heart," said Hans. "But I will tell you one thing — you will have a weary task to drag it along." The Horseman got off, took the silver, helped Hans up, put the bridle into his hand, and said : —

"When you want to go very fast, you must smack your lips, and cry 'Jip.'"

Hans was delighted as he sat on the horse and rode merrily on. After a time he thought he should like to go a little faster, so he smacked his lips and cried "Jip." Away went the horse full gallop; Hans held on tightly, but soon he was thrown off, and lay in a ditch by the roadside. His horse would have run away, if a Cowherd had not stopped it. Hans soon came to himself, and got upon his legs again. He was greatly vexed, and said to the Cowherd : —

"This riding is no joke when a man gets on a beast like this, that stumbles and flings him off and tries to break his neck. However, I am off now once for all. I like your cow a great deal better. I could walk along at my ease behind her, and have milk, butter, and cheese every day into the bargain. What would I give to have such a cow!"

"Well," said the Cowherd, "if you are so fond of her, I will change my cow for your horse."

"Done!" said Hans merrily. The Cowherd jumped upon the horse and away he rode. Hans drove his cow quietly, and thought his bargain a very lucky one.

"If I have only a piece of bread — and I certainly shall be able to get that — I can eat my butter and cheese with it. When I am thirsty I can milk my cow and drink the milk. What can I wish for more?"

Now he came to an inn; he halted, and gave away his last penny for a piece of bread, and ate it. Then he drove his cow toward the village where his mother lived. The heat grew greater as noon came on, till at last he found himself on a wide plain; it would take him more than an hour to cross the plain. He began to be so hot and parched that his tongue cleaved to the roof of his mouth.

"I can find a cure for this," thought he; "now I will milk my cow and quench my thirst." So he tied her to the stump of a tree, and held his leathern cap to milk into it; but not a drop was to be had.

While he was trying his luck and doing very ill, the uneasy beast gave him a kick on the head; the kick knocked him down, and there he lay a long time senseless. Luckily a Butcher soon came by, wheeling a pig in a wheelbarrow.

"What is the matter with you?" asked the Butcher, as he helped him up. Hans told him what had happened, and the Butcher gave him some water.

"There, drink and refresh yourself. Your cow will give you no milk; she is an old beast, fit only to be killed and eaten."

"Alas, alas!" said Hans. "Who would have thought it? If I kill her, what would she be good for? I hate cow-beef; it is not tender enough for me. If it were a pig now, I could do something with it; it would at any rate make some sausages."

"Well," said the Butcher, "to please you, I will change, and give you the pig for the cow."

"Heaven reward you for your kindness!" said Hans, as he gave the Butcher the cow. He took the pig off the wheelbarrow, and drove it along, holding it by the string that was tied to its leg.

II.

THE PIG, THE GOOSE, THE GRINDSTONE, AND NOTHING.

So on he jogged, and all seemed now to go well with him. He had met with some ill luck, to be sure, but he was now well repaid. The next person he met was a Farmer carrying a fine white goose under his arm. The Farmer stopped to ask what o'clock it was, and Hans told him all his luck, and how he had made so many good bargains. The Farmer said he was going to take the goose to market.

"Feel," said he, "how heavy it is, and yet it is only eight weeks old. Whoever roasts and eats it may cut plenty of fat off it, it has lived so well."

"You are right," said Hans, as he weighed the goose in his hand; "but my pig is no trifle." Now the Farmer began to look grave, and shook his head.

"Hark ye, my good friend," said he. "Your pig may get you into a scrape. In the village I just came from the squire has had a pig stolen out of his sty. I was very much afraid when I saw you that you had the squire's pig. It will be a bad job if they catch you; the least they will do will be to throw you into the horse pond." Poor Hans was in great fright.

"Good man," he cried, " pray get me out of this scrape. You know the country better than I; take my pig and give me the goose,"

"I ought to have something into the bargain," said the Farmer. "However, I will not be hard upon you, since you are in trouble." Then he took the string in his hand, and drove the pig away by a side path, while Hans went on, free from care.

"After all," thought Hans, "I have the best of the bargain. First, there will be a capital roast; then the fat will keep me in goose-grease for six months; and there are all the soft white feathers. I will put them into my pillow, and then I shall sleep soundly. How happy my mother will be!"

As he came to the last village on the way, he saw a Scissors-grinder with his wheel, working away and singing merrily. Hans stood by looking on for a while, and at last said : —

"You must be well off, Master Grinder, you seem so happy at your work."

"Yes," said the other; "mine is a golden trade; a good grinder never puts his hand into his pocket without finding money. But where did you get that beautiful goose?"

"I did not buy it, but changed a pig for it."

"And where did you get the pig?"

"I gave a cow for it."

" And the cow ? "

" I gave a horse for it."

" And the horse ? "

"I gave a piece of silver as big as my head for that."

" And the silver ? "

" Oh, I worked hard for that for seven long years."

" You have done well so far," said the Grinder. " Now if you could find money in your pocket whenever you put your hand into it, your fortune would be made."

" Very true ; but how is that to be brought about ? "

" You must turn grinder like me. You only want a grindstone ; the rest will come of itself. Here is one that is a little the worse for wear ; I would not ask more than your goose for it ; — will you buy ? "

" How can you ask such a question ? " replied Hans ; " I should be the happiest fellow in the world, if I could have money whenever I put my hand into my pocket. What could I want more? There is the goose ! "

" Now," said the Grinder, as he gave him a common rough stone that lay by his side, " this is a capital stone ; only use it cleverly, and you can make an old nail cut with it." Hans took the stone, and went off with a light heart. His eyes shone for joy, and he said to himself : —

"I must have been born in a lucky hour. Everything I want or wish for comes to me of itself."

Now Hans began to be tired, for he had been traveling ever since daybreak. He was hungry, too, for he had spent his last penny. At last he could go no further, for the stone was very heavy. He dragged himself to the side of a pond; there he meant to drink some water and rest awhile. He laid the stone carefully by his side on the bank, and stooped to drink; but he forgot the stone and pushed it a little; down it went plump into the pond.

For a while he watched it in the deep clear water; then he sprang up for joy, and again fell on his knees and thanked Heaven with tears in his eyes for taking away his only plague, the ugly heavy stone.

"How happy I am!" he cried. "Surely no mortal was ever so lucky as I." Then he got up with a light and merry heart, and walked on, free from all his troubles, till he reached his mother's house.

THE LION AND THE MOUSE.

As a Lion lay asleep, a Mouse, by chance, ran into his mouth. The Lion shut his teeth together and would have eaten him up, but the Mouse begged hard to be let out, saying: —

"If you will let me go, I shall be forever grateful."

The Lion smiled, and let the Mouse out. Not long after, the Mouse had a chance to repay him, for the Lion was caught by some hunters, and bound with ropes to a tree. The Mouse heard him roar and groan, and ran and gnawed the ropes, so that the Lion got free.

Then the Mouse said : —

"You laughed at me once, Lion, as if you could get nothing in return for your kindness to me, but now it is you who owe your life to me."

This fable teaches that there may come sudden changes of fortune, when the strong will owe everything to the weak.

THE LION AND THE BEAR.

A Lion and a Bear chanced to fall upon a Fawn at the same time, and they began to fight for it. They fought so fiercely that at last they fell down, entirely worn out and almost dead.

A Fox, passing that way, saw them stretched out, and the Fawn dead between them. He stole in slyly, seized the Fawn, and ran away with it for his own dinner. When they saw this, they could not stir, but they cried out : —

" What wretches we are to take all this trouble for the Fox ! "

This fable teaches that when two people fall to fighting for something, a third person is apt to get it.

THE HUNTER AND THE WOODCUTTER.

A HUNTER was looking for the tracks of a Lion, and he asked a Woodcutter whom he met if he had seen any tracks of a Lion, and if he knew where the Lion was hid. The Woodcutter said : —

" Oh, I can show you the Lion himself."

Then the Hunter was pale with fright, his teeth chattered, and he said : —

" I only want to see his tracks ; I don't want to see the Lion."

There are those who are brave with words only, and not with deeds.

THE DOG AND THE WOLF.

A DOG was lying asleep in front of a stable. A Wolf suddenly came upon him, and was about to make a meal of him, but the Dog begged for his life, saying :—

" I am lean and tough now; but wait a little, for my master is going to give a feast, and then

I shall have plenty to eat ; I shall grow fat, and make a better meal for you."

So the Wolf agreed, and went away. By and by he came back, and found the Dog asleep on the house-top. He called to him to come down now and do as he had agreed. But the Dog answered : —

"Good Wolf, if you ever catch me again asleep in front of the stable, you had better not wait for the feast to come off."

This fable teaches that wise men, when they escape danger, take care afterwards not to run the same risk.

JACK AND THE BEAN-STALK.

I.

THE BEANS ARE PLANTED.

In the days of King Alfred a poor woman was living in a country village in England. She had an only son, Jack, who was a good-natured, idle boy. She was too easy with him. She never set him at work, and soon there was nothing left them but their cow. Then the mother began to weep and to think that she had brought up her boy very ill.

"Cruel boy!" she said. "You have at last made me a beggar. I have not money enough to buy a bit of bread. We cannot starve. We must sell the cow, and then, what shall we do?"

At first Jack felt very badly and wished he had done better. But soon he began to think what fun it would be to sell the cow. He begged his mother to let him go with the cow at once to the nearest village. She was not very willing. She did not believe Jack knew enough to sell a cow, but at last she gave him leave.

Off went Jack with the cow. He had not gone far when he met a Butcher.

"Where are you going with your cow?" asked the Butcher.

"I am going to sell it," said Jack. The Butcher, as they talked, held his hat in his hand and shook it. Jack looked into the hat and saw some odd-looking beans. The Butcher saw him eye them. He knew how silly Jack was, so he said to him : —

" Well, if you wish to sell your cow, sell her to me. I will give you all these beans for her."

Jack thought this a fine bargain. He gave the Butcher the cow and took the beans. He ran all the way home and could hardly wait to reach the house. He called out to his mother to see what he had got for the cow.

When the poor woman saw only a few beans, she burst into tears. She was so vexed that she threw the beans out of the window. She did not even cook them for supper. They had nothing else to eat and they went to bed hungry.

Jack awoke early the next morning and thought it very dark. He went to the window and could hardly see out of it, for it was covered with something green. He ran down stairs and into the garden. There he saw a strange sight.

The beans had taken root and shot up toward the clouds. The stalks were as thick as trees, and were wound about each other. It was like a green ladder, and Jack at once wished to climb to the top.

He ran in to tell his mother, but she begged him not to climb the bean-stalk. She did not know what would happen. She was afraid to have him go. Who ever saw such bean-stalks before?

But Jack had set his heart on climbing, and he told his mother not to be afraid. He would soon see what it all meant. So up he climbed. He climbed for hours. He went higher and higher, and at last, quite tired out, he reached the top.

II.

JACK CAPTURES A HEN.

Then he looked about him. It was all new. He had never seen such a place before. There was not a tree or plant; there was no house or shed. Some stones lay here and there, and there were little piles of earth. He could not see a living person.

Jack sat down on one of the stones. He wished he were at home again. He thought of his mother. He was hungry, and he did not know where to get anything to eat. He walked and walked, and hoped he might see a house.

He saw no house, but at last he saw, far off, a lady walking alone. He ran toward her, and when he came near, he pulled off his cap and made a bow. She was a beautiful lady, and she carried in her hand a stick. A peacock of fine gold sat on top of the stick.

The lady smiled and asked Jack how he came there. He told her all about the bean-stalk. Then she said : —

"Do you remember your father?"

"No," said Jack. "I do not know what became of him. When I speak of him to my mother, she cries, but she tells me nothing."

"She dare not," said the lady, "but I will tell you. I am a fairy. I was set to take care of your father, but one day I was careless. So I lost my power for a few years, and just when your father needed me most I could not help him, and he died."

Jack saw that she was very sorry as she told this story, but he begged her to go on.

"I will," she said, "and you may now help your mother. But you must do just as I tell you."

Jack promised.

"Your father was a good, kind man. He had a good wife, he had money, and he had friends. But he had one false friend. This was a Giant. Your father had once helped this Giant, but the Giant was cruel. He killed your father and took all his money. And he told your mother she must never tell you about your father. If she did, then the Giant would kill her and kill you too.

"You were a little child then, and your mother carried you away in her arms. I could not help her at the time, but my power came back to me yesterday. So I made you go off with the cow, and I made you take the beans, and I made you climb the bean-stalk.

"This is the land where the Giant lives. You must find him and rid the world of him. All that he has is yours, for he took it from your father. Now go. You must keep on this road till you see a great house. The Giant lives there. I cannot tell you what you must do next, but I will help you when the time comes; but you must not tell your mother anything."

The fairy disappeared and Jack set out. He walked all day, and when the sun set, he came to

the Giant's house. He went up to it and saw
a plain woman by the door. This was the Giant's wife. Jack spoke to her and asked her
if she would give him something to eat and a
place where he could sleep.

"What!" she said. "Do you not know?
My husband is a Giant. He is away now, but
he will be back soon. Sometimes he walks fifty
miles in a day to see if he can find a man or
a boy. He eats people. He will eat you if he
finds you here."

Jack was in great fear, but he would not
give up. He asked the Giant's wife to hide him
somewhere in the house. She was a kind woman, so she led him in. They went through
a great hall, and then through some large rooms.
All was grand and gloomy. They came to a
dark passage, and went through it. There was
a little light, and Jack could see bars of iron
at the side. Behind the bars were wretched
people. They were the prisoners of the Giant.

Poor Jack thought of his mother and wished
himself at home again. He began to think
the Giant's wife was as bad as the Giant, and
had brought him in to shut him up here. Then
he thought of his father and marched boldly on.

They came to a room where a table was set.
Jack sat down and began to eat. He was very
hungry and soon forgot his fears. But while

he was eating, there came a loud knock at the outside door. It was so loud that the whole house shook. The Giant's wife turned pale.

"What shall I do?" she cried. "It is the Giant. He will kill you and kill me too! What shall I do?"

"Hide me in the oven," said Jack. There was no fire under it, and Jack lay in the oven and looked out. The Giant came in and scolded his wife, and then he sat down and ate and drank for a long time. Jack thought he never would finish. At last the Giant leaned back in his chair and called out in a great loud voice: —

"Bring me my hen!"

His wife brought a beautiful hen and placed it on the table.

"Lay!" roared the Giant, and the hen laid an egg of solid gold.

"Lay another!" and the hen laid another. So it went on. Each time the hen laid a larger egg than before. The Giant played with the hen for some time. Then he sent his wife to bed, but he sat in his chair. Soon he fell asleep, and then Jack crept out of the oven and seized the hen. He ran out of the house and down the road. He kept on till he came again to the bean-stalk, and climbed down to his old home.

III.

THE GIANT'S MONEY-BAGS.

JACK's mother was very glad to see him. She was afraid that he had come to some ill end.

"Not a bit of it, mother," said he. "Look here!" and he showed her the hen. "Lay!" he said to the hen, and the hen laid an egg of gold.

Jack and his mother now had all they needed, for they had only to tell the hen to lay, and she laid her golden egg. They sold the egg and had money enough. But Jack kept thinking of his father, and he longed to make another trial. He had told his mother about the Giant and his wife, but he had said nothing about the fairy and his father.

His mother begged Jack not to climb the bean-stalk again. She said the Giant's wife would be sure to know him, and he never would come back alive. Jack said nothing, but he put on some other clothes and stained his face and hands another color. Then one morning he rose early and climbed the bean-stalk a second time.

He went now straight to the Giant's house. The Giant's wife was again at the door, but she did not know him. He begged for food and a place to sleep. She told him about the Giant, and then she said : —

" There was once a boy who came just as you have come. I let him in, and he stole the Giant's hen and ran away. Ever since the Giant has been very cruel to me. No, I cannot let you come in."

But Jack begged so hard that at last she let him in. She led him through the house, and he saw just what he saw before. She gave him something to eat, and then she hid him in a closet. The Giant came along in his heavy boots. He was so big, that the house shook. He sat by the fire for a time. Then he looked about and said : —

" Wife, I smell fresh meat."

" Yes," she said. " The crows have been fly-ing about. They left some raw meat on top of the house." Then she made haste and got some supper for the Giant. He kept talking about his hen, and was very cross. So it went on as before. The Giant ate and drank. Then he called to his wife : —

" Bring me something. I want to be amused. You let that rascal steal my hen. Bring me something."

" What shall I bring ? " she asked meekly.

" Bring me my money - bags ; they are as heavy as anything." So she tugged two great bags to the table. One was full of silver and one was full of gold. The Giant sent his wife to bed. Then he untied the strings, emptied his bags, and counted his money. Jack watched him, and said to himself : —

"That is my father's money."

By and by the Giant was tired. He put the money back into the bags and tied the strings, and then he went to sleep. He had a dog to watch his money, but Jack did not see the dog. So when the Giant was sound asleep, Jack came out of the closet and laid hold of the bags.

At this the dog barked, and Jack thought his end had come. But the Giant did not wake, and Jack just then saw a bit of meat. He gave it to the dog, and while the dog was eating it, Jack took the two bags and was off.

IV.

THE HARP.

It was two whole days before he could reach the bean-stalk, for the bags were very heavy. Then he climbed down with them. But when he came to his house the door was locked. No one was inside, and he knew not what to do.

After a while he found an old woman who

showed him where his mother was. She was very sick in another house. The poor thing had been made ill by Jack's going away, but now that he had come back, she began to get well, and soon she was in her own house again.

Jack said no more about the Giant and the bean-stalk. For three years he lived with his mother. They had money enough, and all seemed well. But Jack could not forget his father. He sat all day before the bean-stalk. His mother tried hard to amuse him, and she tried to find out what he was thinking about. He did not tell her, for he knew all would then go wrong.

At last he could bear it no longer. He had changed in looks now, and he changed himself still more. Then, one bright summer morning, very early in the day, he climbed the bean-stalk once more. The Giant's wife did not know him when he came to the door of the house, but he had hard work to make her let him in.

This time he was hidden in the copper boiler. The Giant again came home, and was in a great rage.

"I smell fresh meat!" he cried. His wife could do nothing with him, and he began to go about the room. He looked into the oven, and into the closet, and then he came to the great boiler. Jack felt his heart stop. He thought now his end had come, surely. But the Giant did not lift the lid. He sat down by the fire and had his supper.

When supper was over, the Giant told his wife to bring his harp. Jack peeped out of the copper and saw a most beautiful harp. The Giant placed it on the table, and said : —

"Play !"

Jack never heard such music as the harp played. No hands touched it. It played all by itself. He thought he would rather have this harp than the hen or all the money. By and by the harp played the Giant to sleep. Then Jack crept out and seized the harp. He was running off with it, when some one called loudly : —

"Master ! Master !"

It was the harp, but Jack would not let it go. The Giant started up, and saw Jack with the harp running down the road.

"Stop, you rascal !" he shouted. " You stole my hen and my money-bags. Do you steal my harp ? I 'll catch you, and I 'll break every bone in your body ! "

"Catch me if you can !" said Jack. He knew he could run faster than the Giant. Off they went, Jack and the harp, and the Giant after them. Jack came to the bean-stalk. The harp was all the while playing music, but now Jack said : —

"Stop!" and the harp stopped playing. He hurried down the bean-stalk with the harp. There sat his mother, by the cottage, weeping.

"Do not cry, mother," he said. "Quick, bring me a hatchet! Make haste!" He knew there was not a minute to spare. The Giant was already coming down. He was half-way down when Jack took his hatchet and cut the bean-stalk down, close to its roots. Over fell the bean-stalk, and down came the Giant upon the ground. He was killed on the spot.

In a moment the fairy was seen. She told Jack's mother everything, and how brave he had been. And that was the end. The bean-stalk never grew again.

THE WOLF AND THE GOAT.

A Wolf saw a Goat feeding upon the edge of a steep rock, where he could not get at her.

"Come down lower," said he; "the grass is much richer here where I am."

"Thank you, good sir," said the Goat; "you are not inviting me to feed myself, but to be food for you."

THE STAG AND THE LION.

A THIRSTY Stag came to a spring to drink; as he drank, he looked into the water and saw himself. He was very proud of his horns, when he saw how big they were and what branches they had; but he looked at his feet, and took it hard that they should be so thin and weak.

Now, while he was thinking about these things, a Lion sprang out and began to chase him. The Stag turned and ran, and as he was very fleet he outran the Lion so long as they were on the open plain; but when they came to a piece of woods, the Stag's horns became caught in the branches of the trees. He could not run, and the Lion caught up with him.

As the Lion fell upon him with his claws, the Stag cried out : —

"What a wretch am I! I was made safe by the very parts I scorned, and have come to my end by the parts I gloried in!"

THE FARMER'S SONS.

A FARMER's Sons once fell out. The Farmer tried to make peace between them, but though he used many words, he could do nothing. Then he bade them bring him some sticks. These he tied together into a bundle, and gave the bundle in turn to each of his Sons, and told him to break it. Each son tried, but could not.

Then he untied the bundle and gave them each one stick to break; this they did easily, and he said: "So is it with you, my Sons. If you are all of the same mind, your enemies can do you no harm; but if you quarrel, they will easily get the better of you."

THE FOX IN THE WELL.

An unlucky Fox dropped into a well, and cried out for help. A Wolf overheard him, and looked down to see what the matter was.

"Ah!" says the Fox, "pray lend a hand, friend, and get me out of this."

"Poor creature," says the Wolf, "how did this come about? How long hast thou been here? Thou must be mighty cold."

"Come, come," says the Fox, "this is no time for pitying and asking questions; get me out of the well first, and I will tell you all about it afterwards."

THE TWO PACKS.

Every man carries two Packs, one in front, the other behind, and each is full of faults. But the one in front holds other people's faults, the one behind holds his own. And so it is that men do not see their own faults at all, but see very clearly the faults of others.

PUSS IN BOOTS.

I.

PUSS GOES A-HUNTING.

THERE was once an old miller, and when he came to die he left nothing to his three sons except his mill, an ass, and a cat. The eldest son took the mill, the second son took the ass, and so the cat fell to the youngest. This poor fellow looked very sober, and said : —

"What am I to do? My brothers can take care of themselves with a mill and an ass ; but I can only eat the cat and sell his skin. Then what will be left? I shall die of hunger." The cat heard these words and looked up at his master.

"Do not be troubled," he said. "Only give me a bag and get me a pair of boots, and I will soon show you what I can do."

The young man did not see what the cat could do, but he knew he could do many strange things. He had seen him hang stiff by his hind legs as if he were dead ; he had seen him hide himself in the meal tub. Oh! the cat was a wise one! Besides, what else was there for the young man to do?

So he got for the cat a bag and a pair ᵣe

boots. Puss drew on the boots and hung the
bag about his neck. Then he took hold of the
two strings of the bag with his fore paws and
set off for a place where there were some rabbits.

He filled his bag with bran and left the mouth
of the bag open. Then he lay down, shut his
eyes, and seemed to be sound asleep. Soon a
young rabbit smelled the bran and saw the open
bag. He went headlong into it, and at once the
cat drew the strings and caught the rabbit.

Puss now went to the palace, and asked to
speak to the king. So he was brought before
the king, and he made a low bow and said : —

"Sire, this is a rabbit which my master bade
me bring to you."

"And who is your master?"

"He is the Marquis of Carabas," said the cat,
bowing low. This was a title which Puss took
it into his head to give to his master.

"Tell your master that I accept his gift,"
said the king, and Puss went off in his boots.
In a few days he hid himself with his bag in a
cornfield. This time he caught two partridges,
and carried them as before to the king. The
king sent his thanks to the Marquis of Carabas,
and made a present to Puss.

So things went on for some time. Every
week Puss brought some game to the king, and
ιǝ king began to think the Marquis of Carabas
see

a famous hunter. Now it chanced that the
king and his daughter were about to take a
drive along the banks of a river. Puss heard of
it and went to his master.

"Master," said he, "do just as I tell you, and
your fortune will be made. You need only go
and bathe in the river at a spot I shall point
out, and leave the rest to me."

"Very well," said his master   He did as the
cat told him, but he did not know what it all
meant. While he was in the river, the king
and the princess drove by. Puss jumped out of
the bushes and began to bawl : —

"Help! help! the Marquis of Carabas is
drowning! save him!" The king heard and
looked out of his carriage. There he saw the
cat that had brought him so much game, and he
bade his men run to help the Marquis. When
he was out of the river, Puss came forward, and
told what had happened.

"My master was bathing and some robbers
came and stole his clothes. I ran after them
and cried 'Stop thief!' but they got away.
Then my master was carried beyond his depth,
and would have drowned, if you had not come
by with your men."

At this the king bade one of his servants ride
back and bring a fine suit of clothes for the
Marquis, and they all waited. So, at last, the

Marquis of Carabas came up to the carriage, dressed much more finely than he ever had been in his life. He was a handsome fellow, and he looked so well that the king at once bade him enter the carriage.

II.

PUSS AND THE LION.

Puss now had things quite to his mind. He ran on before and came to a meadow, where some men were mowing grass. He stopped before them, and said : —

"I say, good folks, the king is coming this way. You must tell him that this field belongs to the Marquis of Carabas, or you shall all be chopped as fine as mince-meat." When the carriage came by, the king put his head out, and said to the men : —

"This is good grass land. Who owns it ?"

"The Marquis of Carabas," they all said, for Puss had thrown them into a great fright.

"You have a fine estate, Marquis," said the king.

"Yes, Sire," he replied, tossing his head; "it pays me well." Puss still ran before the carriage and came soon to some reapers.

"I say," he cried, "mind you tell the king

that all this grain belongs to the Marquis of Carabas, or you shall all be chopped as fine as mince-meat." The king now came by and asked the reapers who owned the grain they were cutting.

"The Marquis of Carabas," they said. So it went on. Puss bade the men in the fields call the Marquis of Carabas their lord, or it would go hard with them. The king was amazed. The Marquis took it all with a grand air, and it was easy to see that he was a very rich and great man indeed. The princess sat in the corner of the carriage, and thought the Marquis no mean fellow.

At last they drew near the castle of the one who really owned all the fields they had passed through. Puss asked about him and found he was a monster who made every one about him very much afraid. Puss sent in word that he should like to pay his respects, and the monster bade him come in.

"I have been told," said Puss, "that you can change yourself into any kind of animal. They say you can even make yourself a lion."

"To be sure I can," said the monster, sharply. "Do you not believe it? Look, and you shall see me become a lion at once." When Puss saw a lion before him, he was thrown into a great fright, and got as far away as he could. There he stayed till the lion became a monster again.

"That was dreadful!" said Puss. "I was nearly dead with fear. But it must be much harder to make yourself small. They do say that you can turn into a mouse, but I do not believe it."

"Not believe it!" cried the monster. "You shall see!" So he made himself at once into a mouse, and began running over the floor. In a twinkling Puss pounced upon him and gave him one shake. That was the end of the monster.

By this time the king had reached the gates of the castle, and thought he would like to see so fine a place. Puss heard the wheels and ran down just as the king drove up to the door.

"Welcome!" he said, as he stood on the steps of the castle. "Welcome to the castle of the Marquis of Carabas!"

"What! my lord Marquis," said the king, "does this castle, too, belong to you? I never saw anything so fine. I should really like to enter."

"Your majesty is welcome!" said the young man, bowing low, taking off the cap which the king had given him. Then he gave his hand to the princess, and they went up the steps. Puss danced before them in his boots.

They came into a great hall, and there they found a feast spread. The monster had asked some friends to dine with him that day, but the news went about that the king was at the castle, and so they dared not go.

The king was amazed at all he saw, and the princess went behind him, just as much pleased. The Marquis of Carabas said little. He held his head high and played with his sword.

When dinner was over, the king took the marquis one side, and said : —

" You have only to say the word, my lord Marquis, and you shall be the son-in-law of your king."

So the marquis married the princess, and Puss in Boots became a great lord, and hunted mice for mere sport, just when he pleased.

THE FARMER AND THE STORK.

A Farmer set a net in his field to catch the Cranes that were eating his grain. He caught the Cranes, and with them a Stork also. The Stork was lame, and begged the Farmer to let him go.

" I am not a Crane," he said. " I am a Stork. I am a very good bird, and take care of my father and mother. Look at the color of my skin ; it is not the same as the Crane's."

But the Farmer said : " I do not know how that is. I caught you with the Cranes, and with the Cranes you must die."

It is well to keep out of the way of wicked people, lest we fall into the trap with them.

THE FOX AND THE GRAPES.

A Fox, who was hungry, found some bunches of grapes upon a vine high up a tree. He longed to get at them, but could not. So he left them hanging there and went off, saying to himself : —

"They are sour grapes."

That is what people sometimes do when they cannot get what they want; they make believe that what they want is good for nothing.

THE GOOSE THAT LAID GOLDEN EGGS.

There was a man who once had a Goose that always laid golden eggs, one every day in the year.

Now, he thought there must be gold inside of her; so he wrung her neck and laid her open, and found that she was exactly like all other geese. He thought to find riches, and lost the little he had.

This fable teaches that one should be content with what he has, and not be greedy.

THE DOG AND HIS IMAGE.

A Dog, with a bit of meat in his mouth, was crossing a river. Looking down he saw his image in the water, and thought it was another dog, with a bigger piece. So he dropped what he had, and jumped into the water after the other piece. Thus he lost both pieces: the one he really had, which he dropped; and the one he wanted, which was no piece at all.

This is a good fable for greedy people.

THE MAN AND THE LION.

A Lion was once going along the road with a Man, and each was telling large stories. By and by they came upon the statue, by the roadside, of a man with his hand upon a lion's throat. The Man pointed to it, and said : —

"There! see how much stronger we are than you! We are the masters of animals."

But the Lion said quickly : —

"That is the way these things are done by you; but if lions knew how to carve in stone, you would see the lion there with his paw on the man's neck."

TOM THUMB.

I.

TOM IS SOLD FOR A BARGAIN.

A POOR woodman once sat by the fire in his cottage, and his wife sat by his side, spinning.

"How lonely it is," said he, "for you and me to sit here by ourselves without any children to play about and amuse us."

"What you say is very true," said his wife, as she turned her wheel. "How happy should I be, if I had but one child. If it were ever so small, if it were no bigger than my thumb, I should be very happy and love it dearly."

Now it came to pass that the good woman had her wish, for some time afterward she had a little boy who was healthy and strong, but not much bigger than her thumb. So they said : —

"Well, we cannot say we have not got what we wished for, and, little as he is, we will love him dearly!" and they called him Tom Thumb. They gave him plenty to eat, yet he never grew bigger, but remained just the same size as when he was born; still his eyes were sharp and sparkling, and he soon showed himself to be a bright little fellow, who always knew what he was about.

One day the woodman was getting ready to go into the wood to cut fuel, and he said : —

"I wish I had some one to bring the cart after me, for I want to make haste."

"O father," cried Tom, "I will take care of that ; the cart shall be in the wood by the time you want it." The woodman laughed and said : —

"How can that be ? You cannot reach up to the horse's bridle."

"Never mind that, father. If my mother will only harness the horse, I will get into his ear, and tell him which way to go."

"Well," said the father, "we will try for once."

When the time came, the mother harnessed the horse to the cart, and put Tom into his ear. There the little man sat and told the beast how to go, crying out, "Go on," and "Stop," as he wanted. So the horse went on just as if the woodman were driving it himself.

It happened that the horse fell to trotting too fast, and Tom called out, "Gently, gently." Just then two strangers came up.

"How odd it is," one of them said. "There is a cart going along, and I hear a carter talking to the horse, but I see no one."

"That is strange," said the other. "Let us follow the cart and see where it goes." They went on into the wood, and came at last to the place where the woodman was. The cart drove up and Tom said : —

"See, father, here I am with the cart, safe and sound. Now, take me down."

So his father took hold of the horse with one hand, and lifted his son down with the other. He put him on a little stick, where he was as merry as you please. The two strangers looked on and saw it all, and did not know what to say for wonder. At last one took the other aside and said : —

"That little chap will make our fortune if we can get him, and carry him about from town to town as a show. We must buy him." Then they went to the woodman and asked him what he would take for the little man. "He will be better off with us than with you," they said.

"I'll not sell him at all," said the father. "My own flesh and blood is dearer to me than all the silver and gold in the world."

But Tom heard what was said, and crept up his father's coat to his shoulder, and spoke in his ear : —

"Take the money, father, and let them have me. I'll soon come back to you." So the woodman at last agreed to sell Tom Thumb to the strangers for a large piece of gold.

"Where do you like to sit?" one of them asked Tom.

"Oh, put me on the rim of your hat; that will be a nice place for me. I can walk about there and see the country as we go along."

They did as he wished. Tom took leave of his father, and went off with the two strangers. They kept on their way till it began to grow dark. Then Tom said : —

"Let me get down, I am tired." So the man took off his hat, and set him down on a lump of earth in a ploughed field, by the side of the road. But Tom ran about among the furrows, and at last slipped into an old mouse-hole.

"Good-night, masters. I'm off," said he. "Look sharp after me next time." They ran to the place and poked the ends of their sticks into the mouse-hole, but all in vain. Tom crawled farther in. They could not get him, and as it was now quite dark they went away very cross.

II.

HOW TOM FRIGHTENED THE THIEVES.

WHEN Tom found they were gone, he crept out of his hiding-place.

"How dangerous it is," said he, "to walk about in this ploughed field. If I were to fall from one of those big lumps I should surely break my neck." At last, by good luck, he found a large, empty snail-shell.

" This is lucky," said he. " I can sleep here very well," and in he crept. Just as he was falling asleep he heard two men pass by, and one said to the other : —

" How shall we manage to steal that rich farmer's silver and gold ?"

" I 'll tell you !" cried Tom.

" What noise was that? I am sure I heard some one speak," said the thief. He was in a great fright. They both stood listening, and Tom spoke up : —

" Take me with you, and I will soon show you how to get the farmer's money."

" But where are you ?"

" Look about on the ground, and listen where the sound comes from."

" What a little chap ! What can you do for us ?"

" Why, I can get between the iron window bars, and throw you out whatever you want."

" That is a good thought. Come along ; we will see what you can do."

When they came to the farmer's house, Tom slipped through the bars into the room, and then called out as loud as he could : —

" Will you have all that is here ?"

" Softly, softly !" said the thieves. " Speak low, or you will wake somebody."

Tom made as if he did not understand them, and bawled out again : —

"How much will you have? Shall I throw it all out?"

Now the cook lay in the next room, and hearing a noise, she raised herself in her bed and listened. But the thieves had been thrown into a fright and had run away. By and by they plucked up courage, and said: —

"That little fellow is only trying to make fools of us." So they came back and spoke low to him, saying: "Now let us have no more of your jokes, but throw out some of the money." Then Tom called out again as loud as he could: —

"Very well! Hold your hands; here it comes."

The cook heard this plainly; she sprang out of bed, and ran to open the door. The thieves were off as if a wolf were after them, and the cook could see nothing in the dark. So she went back for a light, and while she was gone, Tom slipped off into the barn.

The cook looked about and searched every hole and corner, but found nobody; she went back to bed, and thought she must have been dreaming with her eyes open. Tom crawled about in the hayloft, and at last found a good place to rest in. He meant to sleep till daylight, and then find his way home to his father and mother.

III.

INSIDE A COW.

Poor Tom Thumb! his troubles were only begun. The cook got up early to feed the cows. She went straight to the hayloft, and carried away a large bundle of hay, with the little man in the middle of it fast asleep. He slept on and did not wake till he found himself in the mouth of a cow. She had taken him up with a mouthful of hay.

"Dear me," said he, "how did I manage to tumble into the mill?" But he soon found out where he really was, and he had to keep all his wits about him, or he would have fallen between the cow's teeth, and then he would have been crushed to death. At last he went down into her stomach.

"It is rather dark here," said he; "they forgot to build windows in this room to let the sun in; a candle would be no bad thing." Thus he made the best of his bad luck, but he did not like his resting place at all. The worst of it was, that more and more hay was always coming down, and there was less and less room to turn round in. At last he cried out as loud as he could : —

"Don't bring me any more hay! don't bring

me any more hay!" The cook happened just then to be milking the cow. She heard some one speak, but she saw nobody. Yet she was sure it was the same voice she had heard in the night. It put her into such a fright that she fell off her stool and upset her milk-pail. She ran off as fast as she could to the farmer, and said : —

"Sir, sir, the cow is talking." But the farmer said : —

"Woman, thou art surely mad." Still, he went with her into the cow-house, to see what was the matter. Just as they went in, Tom cried out again : —

"Don't bring me any more hay! don't bring me any more hay!" Then the farmer was in a fright. He was sure the cow must be mad, so he gave orders to have her killed at once. The cow was killed, and the stomach with Tom in it was thrown into the barnyard.

IV.

SAFE AT HOME AGAIN.

Tom soon set himself to work to get out, and that was not a very easy task. But at last, just as he made room to get his head out, a new ill befell him. A hungry wolf was prowling about, and at that moment seized the stomach with Tom in it, and swallowed it. Off he ran, but Tom was not cast down. He began to chat with the wolf, and called out : —

"My good friend, I can show you a famous treat."

"Where is that?"

"In the house near the wood. You can crawl through the drain into the kitchen, and there you will find cakes, ham, beef, and everything that is nice." Now, this was the house where Tom Thumb lived. The wolf did not need to be asked twice. That very night he went to the house and crawled through the drain into the kitchen, and there he ate and drank to his heart's content.

After a while he had eaten so much that he was ready to go away. But now he could not squeeze through the drain. This was just what Tom had thought of, and the little chap set up a great shout.

"Will you be quiet?" said the wolf. "You will wake everybody in the house."

"What is that to me?" said the little man. "You have had your frolic; now I have a mind to be merry myself;" and he began again to sing and shout as loud as he could.

The woodman and his wife were awakened by the noise, and peeped through a crack into the kitchen. When they saw a wolf there, you may be sure they were in a great fright. The woodman ran for his axe, and gave his wife a scythe.

"Now, do you stay behind," said the woodman. "When I have knocked the wolf on the head, you run at him with the scythe." Tom heard all this, and said : —

"Father! father! I am here. The wolf has swallowed me."

"Now, Heaven be praised!" said the woodman. "We have found our dear child again. Do not use the scythe, wife, for you may hurt him." Then he aimed a great blow, and struck the wolf on the head, and killed him at once. They opened him, and set Tom Thumb free.

"Ah!" said his father, "what fears we have had for you!"

"Yes, father," he answered. "I have traveled all over the world since we parted, and now I am very glad to get fresh air again."

"Why, where have you been?"

"I have been in a mouse-hole, in a snail-shell, down a cow's throat, and inside the wolf, and yet here I am again, safe and sound."

"Well, well," said his father. "We will not sell you again for all the riches in the world."

So they hugged and kissed their dear little son, and gave him plenty to eat and drink, and bought him new clothes, for his old ones had been quite spoiled on his journey.

BELLING THE CAT.

THERE was a sly Cat in a house, and the Mice were so plagued with her at every turn, that they called a council to advise some way by which they might guard against being caught by her.

" If you will be ruled by me," says one of the Mice, " there's nothing like hanging a bell about the Cat's neck, to give warning beforehand when Puss is coming." They all thought that a capital plan.

" Well," says another, " and now we are agreed upon the bell, say, who shall hang it upon the Cat's neck ?" But there was no one ready to bell the Cat.

THE FROG AND THE OX.

AN Ox, grazing in a swampy meadow, chanced to set his foot among a number of young Frogs, and crushed nearly all to death. One that escaped ran off to his mother with the dreadful news.

" Oh, mother," said he, " it was a beast, such a big, four-footed beast, that did it ! "

"Big?" said the old Frog. "How big? Was it as big" — and she puffed herself out — "as big as this?"

"Oh, a great deal bigger than that."

"Well, was it so big?" and she swelled herself out yet more.

"Indeed, mother, but it was; and if you were to burst yourself you would never reach half its size." The old Frog made one more trial, determined to be as big as the Ox, and burst herself indeed.

THE MILLER, HIS SON, AND THEIR ASS.

A MILLER and his Son were driving their Ass to the fair to sell him. They had not gone far, when they met a troop of girls, returning from the town, talking and laughing.

"Look there!" cried one of them. "Did you ever see such fools, to be trudging along on foot, when they might be riding?" The Miller, when he heard this, bade his Son get up on the Ass, and walked along merrily by his side. Soon they came to a group of old men talking gravely.

"There!" said one of them; "that proves what I was saying. What respect is shown to old age in these days? Do you see that idle young rogue riding, while his father has to walk? Get down, you scapegrace, and let the old man get on!"

Upon this the Son got down from the Ass, and the Miller took his place. They had not gone far when they met a company of women and children.

"Why, you lazy old fellow!" cried several tongues at once. "How can you ride upon the beast, when that poor little lad, there, can hardly keep pace by the side of you?"

So the good-natured Miller took his Son up behind him. They had now almost reached the town.

"Pray, honest friend," said a townsman, "is that Ass your own?"

"Yes," said the Miller.

"I should not have thought so," said the other, "by the way you load him. Why, you two are better able to carry the poor beast than he to carry you."

"Anything to please you," said the Miller. "We can but try." So he and his Son got down from the Ass; then they tied his legs together, and, taking a stout pole, tried to carry him on their shoulders over a bridge that led to the town.

This was so odd a sight that crowds of people ran out to see it, and to laugh at it. The Ass, not liking to be tied, kicked the cords away, and tumbled off the pole into the water. At this the Miller and his Son hung down their heads, and made their way home again, having learned that by trying to please everybody, they had pleased nobody, and lost the Ass into the bargain.

THE WOLF IN SHEEP'S CLOTHING.

A WOLF once clad himself in the skin of a Sheep, and so got in among the flock, where he made way with a good many of them. At last the Shepherd found him out, and hanged him upon a tree, as a warning to other wolves.

Some Shepherds going by saw the Wolf hanging, and thought it was a Sheep, and wondered why the Shepherd should hang a Sheep. So they asked him, and he answered: "I hang a Wolf when I catch him, even though he be dressed in a Sheep's clothes."

THE ARAB AND HIS CAMEL.

ONE cold night, as an Arab sat in his tent, a Camel gently thrust the flap of the tent aside, and looked in.

"I pray thee, master," he said, "let me but put my head within the tent, for it is cold without."

"By all means, and welcome," said the Arab

cheerfully; and the Camel, moving forward, stretched his head into the tent.

"If I might but warm my neck, also," he said, presently.

"Put also your neck inside," said the Arab. Soon the Camel, who had been turning his head from side to side, said again : —

"It will take but little more room if I place my fore legs within the tent. It is difficult standing without."

"You may also plant your fore legs within," said the Arab, moving a little to make room, for the tent was very small.

"May I not stand wholly within?" asked the Camel, finally. "I keep the tent open by standing as I do."

"Yes, yes," said the Arab. "I will have pity on you as well as on myself. Come wholly inside."

So the Camel came forward and crowded into the tent. But the tent was too small for both.

"I think," said the Camel, "that there is not room for both of us here. It will be best for you to stand outside, as you are the smaller; there will then be room enough for me."

And with that he pushed the Arab a little, who made haste to get outside of the tent.

It is a wise rule to resist the beginnings of evil.

THE FISHERMAN AND THE SPRAT.

A FISHERMAN cast his net, and caught a Sprat. The Sprat begged him to let him go this time, for he was small now, but by and by he would grow to be a big fish, and be worth catching. But the Fisherman said : —

" How foolish it would be for me to let go what I have now, because I might, perhaps, get something better by and by ! "

This fable teaches that a bird in the hand is worth two in the bush.

THE TORTOISE AND THE HARE.

A HARE once made fun of a Tortoise.

" What a slow way you have ! " he said ; " how you creep along ! "

" Do I ? " said the Tortoise. " Try a race with me, and I will beat you."

" You only say that for fun," said the Hare. " But come ! I will race with you. Who will mark off the bounds and give the prize ? "

" Let us ask the Fox," said the Tortoise.

The Fox was very wise and fair ; so he showed them where they were to start, and how far they were to run.

The Tortoise lost no time. She started at once, and jogged straight on.

The Hare knew he could come to the end in two or three jumps; so he lay down and took a nap first. By and by he awoke, and then ran fast; but when he came to the end, the Tortoise was already there!

Slow and steady wins the race.

THE REEDS AND THE OAK.

THE fierce Wind tore up an Oak by its roots, and cast it into the stream. As the Oak floated on the water, it asked the Reeds: —

"How is it that you, who are weak and slender, are not torn up by the roots by this fierce Wind?" And they answered: —

"You fight with the Wind and struggle against it; and so you are rooted up; but we bow before every Wind, and so remain unharmed."

THE COUNTRY MOUSE AND THE TOWN MOUSE.

A COUNTRY Mouse had a friend who lived in a house in town. Now the Town Mouse was invited by the Country Mouse to take dinner with him, and out he went, and sat down to a dinner of barley and wheat.

"Do you know, my friend," said he, "that

you live a mere ant's life out here? Now, I
have plenty at home; come and enjoy the good
things there with me."

So the two set off for town, and there the
Town Mouse showed the other his beans and
meal, his dates, his cheese and fruit and honey.

As the Country Mouse ate, drank, and was
merry, he praised his friend and bewailed his
own poor lot.

But while they were urging each other to eat
heartily, a man suddenly opened the door, and,
frightened by the noise, they crept into a crack.
By and by, when he had gone, they came out
and tasted of some dried figs; when in came
another person to get something that was in the
room, and when they caught sight of him they
ran and hid in a hole.

At that the Country Mouse forgot his hunger,
and fetching a sigh, said to the other : —

" Please yourself, my good friend ; eat all you
want and get rich, — and be in a fright the
whole time. As for me, I am a poor fellow, I
know, who have only barley and wheat, but I
am quite content to live on those, and have
nothing to frighten me."

Those who have the plain things of life are
often better off than the rich.

THE GNAT AND THE BULL.

A GNAT once lit on a Bull's horn, and stayed there a long while.

When he was about to fly away, he asked the Bull if he would like to have him go now.

" Why," said the Bull, " I did not know you were there."

One might answer thus a perfectly useless man, who was neither harmful nor helpful whether he was present or absent.

CINDERELLA; OR THE GLASS SLIPPER.

I.

CINDERELLA IN THE KITCHEN.

ONCE upon a time there lived a man and his wife and one beautiful daughter. The wife fell sick and died, and some time after the father married again, for he needed some one to take care of his child. The new wife appeared very well before the wedding, but afterward she showed a bad temper. She had two children of her own, and they were proud and unkind like their mother. They could not bear their gentle sister, and they made her do all the hard work.

She washed the dishes, and scrubbed the stairs; she swept the floor in my lady's chamber, and took care of the rooms of the two pert misses. They slept on soft beds in fine rooms, and had tall looking-glasses, so that they could admire themselves from top to toe; she lay on an old straw sack in the garret.

She bore all this without complaint. She did her work, and then sat in the corner among the ashes and cinders. So her two sisters gave her the name of Cinderella or the cinder-maid. But for all her shabby dress, Cinderella was really much more beautiful than they; and she surely was more lovely.

Now the King's son gave a ball, and he invited all the rich and the grand. Cinderella's two sisters were fine ladies; they were to go to the ball. Perhaps they would even dance with the prince. So they had new gowns made, and they looked over all their finery.

Here was fresh work for poor Cinderella. She must starch their ruffles and iron their linen. All day long they talked of nothing but their fine clothes.

"I shall wear my red velvet dress," said the elder, "and trim it with my point lace."

"And I," said the younger sister, "shall wear a silk gown, but I shall wear over it a gold brocade, and I shall put on my diamonds. You have nothing so fine."

Then they began to quarrel over their clothes, and Cinderella tried to make peace between them. She had good taste, so she helped them about their dresses, and offered to arrange their hair on the night of the ball.

While she was thus busy, the sisters said to her : —

"And pray, Cinderella, would you like to go to the ball?"

"Nay," said the poor girl; "you are mocking me. It is not for such as I to go to balls."

"True enough," they said with a jeer. "Folks would laugh to see a cinder-maid at a court ball."

Any one else would have dressed their hair ill to spite them for their rudeness. But Cinderella was good-natured, and only took more pains to make them look well.

The two sisters scarcely ate a morsel for two days before the ball. Indeed, it was not very easy for them to eat much, they had laced themselves so tightly. They wished to look thin and graceful. They lost their tempers over and over, and they spent most of the time before their tall glasses. There they turned and turned to see how they looked behind, and how their long trains hung.

At last the evening came, and off they set in a coach. Cinderella watched them till they were out of sight, and then she sat down by the kitchen fire and began to weep.

All at once her fairy godmother appeared, with her wand.

"What are you crying for, my little maid?"

"I wish — I wish," began the poor girl, but her voice was choked with tears.

"You wish that you could go to the ball?" Cinderella nodded.

"Well, then, if you will be a good girl, you shall go. Run quick and fetch me a pumpkin from the garden."

Cinderella flew to the garden and brought back the finest pumpkin she could find. She could not guess what use it would be, but the fairy scooped it hollow, and then touched it with her wand. The pumpkin became at once a splendid gilt coach.

"Now fetch me the mouse-trap from the pantry."

In the mouse-trap were six sleek mice. The fairy opened the door, and as they ran out she touched each with her wand, and it became a gray horse. But what was she to do for a coachman?

"We might look for a rat in the rat-trap," said Cinderella.

"That is a good thought. Run and bring the rat-trap, my dear."

Back came Cinderella with the trap. In it were three large rats. The fairy chose one that had long black whiskers, and she made him the coachman.

"Now go into the garden and bring me six lizards. You will find them behind the water-pot."

These were no sooner brought than, lo! with a touch of the wand they were turned into six footmen, who jumped up behind the coach, as if they had done nothing else all their days. Then the fairy said: —

"Here is your coach and six, Cinderella; your coachman and your footmen. Now you can go to the ball."

"What! in these clothes?" and Cinderella looked down at her ragged frock. The fairy laughed and just touched her with the wand. In a twinkling, her shabby clothes were changed to a dress of gold and silver tissue, and on her bare feet were silk stockings and a pair of glass slippers, the prettiest ever seen.

"Now go to the ball, Cinderella; but re-member, if you stay one moment after midnight, your coach will instantly become a pumpkin, your horses will be mice, your coachman a rat, and your footmen lizards. And you? you will be once more only a cinder-maid in a ragged frock and with bare feet."

II.

CINDERELLA IN THE PALACE.

CINDERELLA promised and drove away in high glee. She dashed up to the palace, and her coach was so fine that the king's son came down the steps of the palace to hand out this unknown princess. He led her to the hall where all the guests were dancing.

The moment she appeared all voices were hushed, the music stopped, and the dancers stood still. Such a beautiful princess had never been seen! Even the king, old as he was, turned to the queen and said : —

" She is the most beautiful being I ever saw — since I first saw you ! "

As for the ladies of the court, they were all busy looking at Cinderella's clothes. They meant to get some just like them the very next day, if possible.

The prince led Cinderella to the place of highest rank, and asked her hand for the next dance. She danced with so much grace that he admired her more and more. Supper was brought in, but the prince could not keep his eyes off the beautiful stranger. Cinderella went and sat by her sisters, and shared with them the fruit which the prince gave her. They were very proud to have her by them, for they never dreamed who she really was.

Cinderella was talking with them, when she heard the clock strike the quarter hour before twelve. She went at once to the king and queen, and made them a low courtesy and bade them good-night. The queen said there was to be another ball the next night, and she must come to that. The prince led her down the steps to her coach, and she drove home.

At the house the fairy sat waiting for Cinderella. The maiden began to tell all that had happened, and was in the midst of her story, when a knock was heard at the door. It was the sisters coming home from the ball. The fairy disappeared, and Cinderella went to the door, rubbing her eyes, as if she had just waked from a nap. She was once more a poor little cinder-maid.

" How late you are ! " she said, as she opened the door.

" If you had been to the ball, you would not have thought it late," said her sisters. " There came the most beautiful princess that ever was seen. She was very civil to us and loaded us with oranges and grapes."

" Who was she ? " asked Cinderella.

" Nobody knew her name. The prince would give his eyes to know."

"Ah! how I should like to see her," said Cinderella. "Oh, do, my Lady Javotte," — that was the name of the elder sister, — "lend me the yellow dress you wear every day, and let me go to the ball and have a peep at the beautiful princess."

"What! lend my yellow gown to a cindermaid! I am not so silly as that."

Cinderella was not sorry to have Javotte say no; she would have been puzzled to know what to do if her sister had really lent her the dress she begged for.

The next night came, and the sisters again went to the court ball. After they had gone, the fairy came as before and made Cinderella ready.

"Now remember," she said, as the coach drove away, "remember twelve o'clock."

Cinderella was even more splendid than on the first night, and the king's son never left her side. He said so many pretty things that Cinderella could think of nothing else. She forgot the fairy's warning; she forgot her promise. Eleven o'clock came, but she did not notice the striking; the half-hour struck, but the prince grew more charming, and Cinderella could hear nothing but his voice; the last quarter — but still Cinderella sat by the prince.

Then the great clock on the tower struck the

first stroke of twelve. Up sprang Cinderella, and, like a frightened fawn, she fled from the room. The prince started to follow her, but she was too swift for him; in her flight, one of her glass slippers fell from her feet, and he stopped to pick it up.

The last stroke of twelve died away, as Cinderella darted down the steps of the palace. In a twinkling the gay lady was gone; only a shabby cinder-maid was running down the steps. The splendid coach and six, driver and footman, — all were gone; only a pumpkin lay on the ground, and a rat, six mice, and six lizards scampered off.

Cinderella reached home, quite out of breath. She had saved nothing of all her finery but one little glass slipper. The prince had its mate, but he had lost the princess. He asked the soldiers at the palace gate if they had not seen her drive away. No; at that hour only a ragged girl had passed out.

Soon the two sisters came home from the ball, and Cinderella asked them if they had again seen the beautiful lady. Yes; she had been at the ball, but she had left suddenly, and no one knew what had become of her. But the prince would surely find her, for he had one of her glass slippers.

They spoke truly. A few days afterward, the

king's son sent a messenger with a trumpet and the slipper through all the city. The messenger sounded his trumpet and shouted that the prince would marry the lady who could wear the glass slipper. So the slipper was first tried on by all the princesses; then by all the duchesses; next by all the persons belonging to the court; but in vain : not one could wear it.

Then it was carried to all the fine houses, and it came at last to the two sisters. They tried with all their might to force a foot into the fairy slipper, but they could not. Cinderella stood by, and said : —

"Suppose I were to try." Her two sisters jeered at her, but the messenger looked at Cinderella. He saw that she was very fair, and, besides, he had orders to try the slipper on the foot of every maiden in the kingdom, if need were.

So he bade Cinderella sit down on a three-legged stool in the kitchen. She put out her little foot, and the slipper fitted like wax. The sisters stood in amaze. Then Cinderella put her hand into her pocket and drew forth the other glass slipper, and put it on her other foot.

The moment that Cinderella did this, the fairy, who stood by unseen, touched her with her wand, and the cinder-maid again became the beautiful, gayly-dressed lady. The sisters saw that she was the same one whom they had seen at the ball. They thought how ill they had treated her all these years, and they fell at her feet and asked her to forgive them.

Cinderella was as good now as she had been when she was a cinder-maid. She freely forgave her sisters, and took them to the palace with her, for she was now to be the prince's wife ; and when the old king and queen died, the prince and Cinderella reigned in their stead.

THE FOX AND THE LION.

A Fox who had never seen a Lion met one by chance, and when he saw him was so afraid that he almost died. When he met him a second time, he was afraid, to be sure, but not as at first. The third time he saw him, the Fox was so bold that he went up to the Lion and spoke to him.

This fable teaches that, when we get used to fearful things, they do not frighten us so much as at first.

THE SLEEPING BEAUTY IN THE WOOD.

I.

THE BEAUTY GOES TO SLEEP.

ONCE upon a time there lived a king and queen who grieved sorely that they had no child. But at last a daughter was born, and the king was overjoyed. He gave a great feast, and asked to it all the fairies in the land, seven in all. He hoped that each would give the child a gift.

In front of each fairy at the table was set a heavy gold plate, and by each plate a gold knife and fork. Just as they sat down to the feast, in came an old fairy who had not been invited. No one knew she was living. Fifty years before she had shut herself up in a tower, and had not been seen since.

The king hurried off to find a gold plate and knife and fork for her also. But nothing could be found so fine as the seven plates which had been made to order for the seven fairies. The old fairy thought herself ill-used and grumbled in a low voice. At that, one of the young fairies feared she meant mischief to the child, and so, when the feast was over, hid herself behind the hangings in the hall. We shall soon see why she did this.

The fairies now began to give gifts to the child, beginning with the youngest. She gave her beauty; the next gave her wit; the third gave her grace; the fourth said she should dance perfectly; the fifth gave her a voice to sing; the sixth said she should play beautifully on the harp.

The turn of the old fairy had now come, and she shook her head wickedly and said the child would grow up, but when she was grown, she would pierce her hand, when spinning, and die of the wound. At this, all the company began to weep, but the fairy who had hidden came forward and said : —

"Be of good cheer, king and queen. Your daughter shall not so die. I cannot entirely undo what my elder has done. The princess must pierce her hand when spinning, but instead of dying she shall fall into a deep sleep. The sleep shall last a hundred years; at the end of that time a king's son will come to wake her."

The king was very sad, but he hoped he might prevent the evil. So he made a law that no one in the kingdom should spin or have a spinning-wheel in the house, under pain of instant death.

All went well for fifteen years. Then it

chanced that the princess was with the king and queen in one of their castles, and was spying about for herself. She came to a little chamber at the top of a tower, and there sat an honest old woman spinning. She was very old and deaf, and had never heard of the king's command.

"What are you doing?" asked the princess.

"I am spinning, my pretty child."

"How charming it is!" said the princess. "How do you do it? Let me try if I can spin." She seized the spindle, but she was hasty and careless, and pierced her hand with its point. She fainted, and the old woman, in great alarm, ran for help. People came running from all sides, but they could not rouse her.

The king heard the noise and came also. Then he saw that the cruel fairy had had her wish. His daughter would not wake for a hundred years. He laid her on the bed in the best room, and stood sadly looking upon her. She was asleep; he could hear her breathe; her cheeks were full of color, but her eyes were closed.

Now the good fairy, who had said the princess should wake in a hundred years, was thousands of miles away at the time. But she knew of it, and came at once in a chariot of fire drawn by dragons. The king came to meet her, his eyes red with weeping.

The good fairy was very wise and saw that the princess would not know what to do if she awoke all alone in the castle, in a hundred years. So this is what she did.

She touched with her wand every one in the castle except the king and the queen. She touched the maids of honor, the gentlemen, the officers, the stewards, cooks, boys, guards, porters, pages, footmen; she touched the horses in the stable, the grooms, the great mastiff in the court-yard, and the tiny lapdog of the princess that was on the bed beside her.

The moment she touched them, they all fell asleep just as they were, not to wake again until the time came for their mistress to do so, and then they all would be ready to wait on her. Even the fire went to sleep, and the roasting-spit before the fire with its fowls ready for roasting.

It was the work of a moment. The king and queen kissed their daughter good-by and left the castle. The king issued a command that no one was to go near the castle. That was needless; for in a quarter of an hour, a wood had grown about it so thick and thorny that nothing could get through it. The castle-top itself could only be seen from afar.

II.

THE BEAUTY WAKES.

AFTER a few years the king and queen died. They had no other child, and the kingdom passed into the hands of a distant family. A hundred years went by. The son of the king who was then reigning was out hunting one day, when he noticed the tower of a castle in the distance. He asked what castle it was.

All manner of answers were given to him. One said it was a fairy castle; another said that a great monster lived there. At last an old man said : —

"Prince, more than fifty years ago I heard my father say that there was in that castle the most beautiful princess ever seen; that she was to sleep for a hundred years, and to be waked at last by the king's son, who was to marry her."

The young prince at these words felt himself on fire. He had not a doubt that he was the one to awaken the princess. He set out at once for the wood, and when he drew near, the trees and thorns opened on one side and the other to offer him a path.

He was on a long, straight road, and at the end was the castle in full view. He turned to

look for his comrades. Not one was to be seen.
The wood had closed again behind him. He
was alone, and all was still about him. Forward
he strode and came to the castle-gate. He
entered the courtyard, and stood still in amazement.

On every side were the bodies of men and
animals. But the faces of the men were rosy;
it was plain that they were asleep. His steps
sounded on the marble floor. He entered the
guardroom. There the guards stood drawn up
in line, with their spears in their hands, but they
did not move. They were fast asleep.

He passed through one room after another;
people were asleep in chairs, on benches, standing, sitting, lying down. He entered a beautiful room, covered with gold, and saw the most
wonderful sight of all.

There lay a maiden so fair that she seemed to
belong to another world. He drew near and
knelt beside her. She did not stir. Her hand
lay on her breast, and he touched his lips to it.

As he did this, her eyes opened and looked at
the young man. She smiled, and said :—

"Have you come, my prince ? I have waited
long for you."

The prince hardly knew how to answer, but
he soon found his voice, and they talked for
hours, and had not then said half that was in
their heads to say.

Now the moment that the princess waked, her little lapdog waked also. The great mastiff in the court-yard awoke; the horses in the stable and the grooms awoke; the footmen, the pages, the porters, the guards, the boys, the cooks, the stewards, the officers, the gentlemen and the maids of honor, all awoke. The fire began to burn again, the spits turned round, and the fowls began to roast.

So, while the prince and the princess forgot the hours in talk, these people began to be hungry. The maids of honor went to the princess to tell her that they all waited for her. Then the prince took the princess by the hand and led her into the hall.

She was dressed in great splendor, but the prince did not hint that she looked as the picture of his great-grandmother looked. He thought her all the more charming for that, but he did not tell her so. The musicians played excellent but old music at supper; and after supper, to lose no time, the prince and princess were married in the chapel of the castle.

The next day they left the castle. All the people followed them down the long path. The wood opened again to let them through. Outside they met the prince's men, and glad they were to see the prince once more. He turned to show them the castle, when, lo! there was no castle to be seen, and no wood.

But the prince and princess rode gaily away, and when the old king and queen died, they reigned in their stead.

THE EAGLE SHOT WITH AN EAGLE'S ARROW.

An Eagle came down out of the sky and lighted on a rock, where he meant to watch for a Hare.

Some one saw the Eagle, and drew a bow and shot him. The arrow drove fast into the Eagle, and the feathers on the arrow stood out plainly before his eyes. They were feathers from an Eagle's wing.

The Eagle closed his eyes, and said : —

"Oh, this is worst of all, — to be killed by an arrow with Eagle's feathers."

This fable teaches how sore a thing it is to be in peril from what belongs to one's self.

THE FOX AND THE STORK.

The Fox invited the Stork to sup with him, and placed a shallow dish on the table. The Stork, with her long bill, could get nothing out of the dish, while the Fox could lap up the food with his tongue; and so the Fox laughed at the Stork.

The Stork, in her turn, asked the Fox to dine with her, and she placed the food in a long-necked jar, from which she could easily feed with her bill, while the Fox could get nothing; and that was tit for tat.

THE SPENDTHRIFT AND THE SWALLOW.

A WILD young fellow, who had spent all his father's money, and had only a cloak left upon his back, when he saw a Swallow flying about before it was time said: "Ah, summer has come! I shall not need my cloak any longer; so I will sell it." But afterwards a storm came, and, when it was past, he saw the poor Swallow dead on the ground. "Ah, my friend!" said he, " you are lost yourself, and you have ruined me."

One Swallow does not make a summer.

THE ANT AND THE GRASSHOPPER.

ON a warm day in summer, an Ant was busy in the field gathering grains of wheat and corn, which he laid up for winter food. A Grass-hopper saw him at work, and laughed at him for toiling so hard, when others were at ease.

The Ant said nothing. But afterwards, when winter came, and the ground was hard, the

Grasshopper was nearly dead with hunger, and came to the Ant to beg something to eat. Then the Ant said to him : —

"If you had worked when I did, instead of laughing at me, you would not now be in need."

THE LION AND THE FOX.

A Lion that had grown old, and had no more strength to forage for food, saw that he must get it by cunning. He went into his den and crept into a corner, and made believe that he was very sick.

All the animals about came in to take a look at him, and, as they came, he snapped them up. Now, when a good many beasts had been caught in this way, the Fox, who guessed the trick, came along. He took his stand a little way from the den, and asked the Lion how he did.

The Lion said he was very sick, and begged him to come into the den and see him.

"So I would," said the Fox, "but I notice that all the footprints point into the den, and there are none that point out."

THE WOLF AND THE SHEPHERD.

A Wolf once walked behind a flock of Sheep, and did them no harm. At first, the Shepherd treated him as an enemy, and kept watch against him ; but when the Wolf made no sign of hurting the Sheep, the Shepherd began to think he was quite as good as a watch-dog.

So one day, when the Shepherd wished to go to the city, he left the Sheep in the care of this quiet Wolf. That was the chance the Wolf wanted, and he made sad havoc in the flock. When the Shepherd came back and saw the Sheep scattered, he said : —

" It serves me right; for why did I trust Sheep to a Wolf ? "

THE FLIES AND THE POT OF HONEY.

A Pot of Honey was upset in the pantry, and the Flies crowded about to eat of it. It was so sticky that they could not get away ; their feet were held fast, so that they could not fly, and they began to choke to death.

" What wretches we are," they cried, " to die just for a moment of pleasure ! "

So it is that greediness is the cause of many evils.

THE CAT, THE MONKEY, AND THE CHEST-NUTS.

A CAT and a Monkey were sitting one day by the hearth, watching some chestnuts which their master had laid down to roast. The chestnuts had begun to burst with the heat, and the Monkey said to the Cat : —

"It is plain that your paws were made to pull out those chestnuts. Your paws are, indeed, exactly like our master's hands."

The Cat was greatly flattered by this speech, and reached forward for the tempting chestnuts; but scarcely had she touched the hot ashes than she drew back with a cry, for she had burned her paw. She tried again, and made out to get one chestnut; then she pulled another, and a third, though each time she singed the hair on her paws.

When she could pull no more, she turned, and found the Monkey had taken this time to crack the chestnuts and eat them.

THE FOX THAT LOST HIS TAIL.

A Fox once got caught in a trap, and lost his tail in getting loose. He was so ashamed that he thought life not worth living. Then he bethought himself and called the rest of the Foxes, and begged them to cut off their tails, telling them that the tail was not only ugly, but a dead weight hung on behind. But one of the Foxes spoke up and said : —

"My good friend, that is all very well, but if it were not to help your case, you never would advise us to cut off our tails."

DICK WHITTINGTON AND HIS CAT.

I.

DICK GOES TO LONDON.

In the olden times there lived in the country, in England, a boy by the name of Dick Whitting-ton. He did not know who his parents were, for he had been born and brought up in the poor-house. There he was cruelly treated, and when he was seven years of age, he ran away and lived by what he could get from kind people.

He heard that the streets of London were paved with gold, and being now a sturdy youth, he set out for the city to make his fortune. He did not know the way, but he fell in with a car-ter, who was bound for London, and he followed the cart. When night came, he helped the carter by rubbing down the horses, and for this he was paid with a supper.

He trudged on thus, day after day, until they came to the famous city. The carter was afraid Dick would hang about him and give him trouble, so he gave him a penny and told him to begone and find some work.

Dick went from street to street, but he knew no one; he was ragged and forlorn, and looked like a beggar. Nobody gave him anything to do. Once in a while some one gave him something to eat, but at last he had nothing.

For two days he went about hungry and almost starved, but he would rather starve than steal. At night, at the end of the second day, he came to a merchant's house in Leadenhall Street, and stood before it, weary and faint. The ill-natured cook saw him and came out and said : —

" Go away from here, or I will kick you away ! " At this, he crept off a little distance and lay down on the ground, for he was too weak to stand. As he lay there, the merchant who lived in the house, came home and stopped to speak to him. He spoke sharply, and told him to get up, that it was a shame for him to be lying there.

Poor Dick got up, and after falling once, through faintness and want of food, made out to say that he was a poor country boy, nearly starved. He would do any work if he might have food.

Mr. Fitzwarren, the merchant, saw in what a wretched plight he was, and took pity on him. He brought him into the house, and bade the servants look after him ; he gave him a place under the cook, and this was the beginning of Dick's fortune. But Dick had a hard time of it. The servants made sport of him, and the ill-natured cook said : —

" Do you know what you are to do ? You are to come under me. So look sharp ; clean the spits and the pans, make the fires, wind up the roasting-jack, and do nimbly all the dirty work I set you about, or else I will break your head with my ladle, and kick you about like a foot-ball."

This was cold comfort, but it was better than starving. What gave him more hope was the kind notice he had from his master's daughter, Mistress Alice. She heard Dick's story from her father, and called for the boy. She asked him questions, and he was so honest in his answers, that she went to her father, and said : —

" That poor boy whom you brought into the house is a good, honest fellow. I am sure he will be very useful. He can clean shoes, and run errands, and do many things which our servants do not like to do."

II.

DICK'S CAT.

So Dick was kept, and a cot bed was given him in the garret. He was up early and worked late. He left nothing undone that was given him to do. For all that, he could not please the cook, who was very sour to him. Still, he bore her blows rather than leave so good a home. Then the cook told tales about him, and tried to get him sent away, but Mistress Alice heard of it; she knew how ill-tempered the cook was, and so she made her father keep Dick.

This was not the whole of Dick Whittington's trouble. The garret where he lay at night had long been empty, and a great number of mice had made their home in it. They ran over Dick's face, and kept up such a racket that he knew not which was worse, the cook by day or the mice by night.

He could only hope that the cook might marry or get tired of the place, and that he might in some way get a cat. It chanced, soon after, that a merchant came to dinner, and as it rained hard, he stayed all night. In the morning Dick cleaned the merchant's shoes and brought them to his door. For this service the merchant gave him a penny.

As he went through the street on an errand that morning, he saw a woman with a cat under her arm. He asked her the price of the cat.

"It is a good mouser," said the woman: "you may have it for a sixpence."

"But I have only a penny," said Dick. The woman found that she really could get nothing more, so she sold the cat to Dick for a penny. He brought it home, and kept it out of the way all day for fear the cook should see it; then at night he took the cat up to the garret, and made her work for her living. Puss soon rid him of one plague.

When Mr. Fitzwarren sent out a ship to trade with far countries, he used to call his servants together, and give each a chance to make some money, by sending out goods in the ship. He thought that thus his ship had better fortune.

Now he was again making a venture, and each of the servants brought something to send; all but Whittington. Mistress Alice saw that he did not come, and she sent for him, meaning to give him some simple goods, that he too might have a share in the venture.

When, after many excuses, he was obliged to appear, he fell on his knees, and prayed them not to jeer at a poor boy. He had nothing he could claim for his own but a cat, which he had bought with a penny given him for cleaning shoes.

Upon this Mistress Alice offered to lay something down for him; but her father told her the custom was for each to send something of his own. So he bade Dick bring his cat, which he did with many tears, and gave him over to the master of the ship.

The cook, and indeed all the servants, after this plagued Dick so sorely, and jeered at him so much for sending his cat, that he could bear it no longer. He said to himself that he would leave the house and try his fortune elsewhere.

III.

BOW BELLS.

HE packed his bundle one night, and the next day, early, set forth to seek his fortune. He left the house behind him, but his heart began to sink. However, he would not turn back, and he kept on, but at last sat down in the field to think.

Just then the Bow Bells, that is, the bells of a church in Bow Street, began to ring merrily. Dick heard them, and as they rang, he fancied he heard them sing, —

" Turn again, Whittington.
Lord Mayor of London."

That was a fine song to hear, and Dick began to pluck up heart again. Still the bells rang. It was very early; no one was yet astir at the merchant's house, and Dick, with new courage, took up his bundle, obeyed the bells, and walked quickly back to the house. He had left the door open, so he crept in and took up his daily task.

Now, about this time, the ship which carried Dick's cat was driven by the winds, and came to a place on the Barbary coast, where the English seldom went. The people received the master of the ship well, and he traded with them. As his wares were new, they were very welcome, and at last the king of that country, being greatly pleased, sent for the captain to come and dine at the palace.

The dinner, after the custom of the country, was not set on a table, but the cloth was laid on the floor. The guests sat cross-legged before the feast. But when the dishes were set down, the smell of the dinner brought a great company of rats, and these rats helped themselves without fear.

The master of the ship was amazed and asked the nobles, who sat there, if it was not very unpleasant to have this swarm of rats.

" Oh," said they, " very much so. The king would give half his wealth to be rid of them.

They not only come to the table, but they make free with his chamber and even his bed."

"Well," said the captain, thinking at once of Dick's cat, "I have an English beast on board my ship which will quickly clear the palace of all the rats."

"Say you so?" said the king, when he heard of this. "For such a thing I will load your ship with gold, diamonds, and pearls." At that the shrewd captain made much of the cat.

"She is the most famous thing in the world," said he. "I cannot spare her, for she keeps my ship clear of rats, or else they would spoil all my goods." But the king would not take no for an answer.

"No price shall part us," he said. So the cat was sent for, and the table was again spread. The rats came as before, but the captain let the cat loose, and she made short work of them. Then she came purring and curling up her tail before the king, as if she would have her reward.

The king was so pleased with the cat, that he gave ten times more for her than for all the goods in the ship. Then the ship sailed away with a fair wind, and arrived safe at London. She was the richest ship that ever entered port.

IV.

LORD MAYOR WHITTINGTON.

THE master took the box of pearls and jewels with him on shore, and went straight to the merchant's house. He gave his account to Mr. Fitzwarren, who was greatly pleased at the fortunate voyage, and called his servants together, to receive each their profit. Then the master showed the box of pearls and jewels, and told the story of Whittington's cat, and how Puss had earned this wealth.

"Call Mr. Whittington," said Mr. Fitzwarren. "I will not take one farthing from him."

Now Dick was in the kitchen cleaning pots and pans. When he was told that the merchant had sent for Mr. Whittington, he thought every one was making fun of him, and he would not go.

At last, since no excuse would be taken, he went as far as the door. The merchant bade him come in, and placed a chair for him. At that poor Dick was sure they were making fun of him, and the tears came into his eyes.

"I am only a simple fellow," he said. "I do not mean harm to any one. Do not mock me."

"Indeed, Mr. Whittington, we are serious with you," said the merchant. "You are a

much richer man than I am," and he gave him
the box of pearls and jewels worth quite three
hundred thousand pounds.

At first Dick could not believe his good fortune. When at last he was persuaded, he fell
upon his knees and thanked God who had been
so good to him. Then he turned to his master
and wished to give him of his wealth, but Mr.
Fitzwarren said : —

"No, Mr. Whittington. I will not take a
penny from you. It is all yours."

At that Dick turned to Mistress Alice, who
also refused. He bowed low, and said : —

"Madam, whenever you please to make choice
of a husband, I will make you the greatest fortune in the world."

Then he gave freely to his fellow servants.
Even to his enemy, the cook, he gave a hundred pounds.

Richard Whittington was now a rich man.
He laid aside his poor clothes, and was dressed
well and handsomely. He had grown strong
and tall in service, and was indeed a fine man
to look upon.

It was seen, too, that he was well behaved and
of a good mind and heart. Mr. Fitzwarren
made him known to the other merchants, and
let him see how business was carried on. Then
seeing that he was honest and good as he was

rich, he told Whittington that he might have his daughter in marriage.

At first, Dick felt himself unworthy of Mistress Alice, but he saw that she looked kindly on him, and he remembered how good she had been to him from the beginning. So he made bold to ask Mistress Alice to be his wife, and they had a grand wedding.

After the wedding was over, Mr. Fitzwarren asked him what he meant to do, and Mr. Whittington said he would like to be a merchant. So the two became partners, and grew to be very rich.

Rich as he was, this merchant never forgot that he was once poor Dick Whittington. The promise of Bow Bells came true, and three times he was chosen Lord Mayor of London. He fed the hungry, and cared for the poor.

When he was Lord Mayor of London the third time, it was his duty to receive King Henry V. and his queen at Guildhall, which was the Mayor's palace. It was just after a famous war with France, which England had won.

The King, at the feast, made the lord mayor a knight, so that now he was Sir Richard Whittington. There was a very pleasant fire on the hearth at the time. It was made of choice wood, and mace and other spices were mixed with the wood. The king praised the fire, and Sir Richard said, — "I will make it still more pleasant." At that he threw upon the flames one piece of paper after another. They were the written promises of the king, to pay for money lent to him by London merchants, when he was carrying on the war. Sir Richard had bought them for sixty thousand pounds. That was the way he paid the king's debt, for now there was nothing to show that the king owed anything.

This is the story of Dick Whittington and his cat. How much is true, and how much was made up, I do not know, for what happened took place five hundred years ago.

THE TRAVELERS AND THE BEAR.

Two friends were walking along the road, when a Bear came suddenly upon them.

One of them got first to a tree, and climbed up into it and hid among the branches.

The other, who was slower, fell flat upon the ground, and made believe that he was dead.

When the Bear came up to him, and poked him with his nose, he held his breath ; for it is said that this animal will not touch a dead man. The Bear went off, and the Man who was in the tree came down, and asked the other what the Bear had whispered.

" He told me," said the other, " not to travel hereafter with friends who would desert me when danger came."

This fable teaches that misfortunes sometimes show which of our friends are true friends.

THE WOLVES AND THE SHEEP.

The Wolves wanted to get into a sheepfold, but the Dogs kept them out. So they tried a trick. They sent grave old fellows to the Sheep, who said : " It is the Dogs who make all this trouble between us. Only send them away, and we can live happily together." The Sheep knew no better than to send the Dogs away, and then the Wolves came in, and easily made an end of the Sheep.

If you listen to your enemy, you will get yourself into trouble.

· THE LARK AND HER YOUNG ONES.

There was a brood of young Larks in a field of corn, which was just ripe, and the mother, looking every day for the reapers, left word, whenever she went out in search of food, that her young ones should tell her all the news they heard.

One day, when she was absent, the master

came to look at his field. "It is full time," said he, "to call in my neighbors and get my corn reaped." When the old Lark came home, the young ones told their mother what they had heard, and begged her to move them at once.

"Time enough," said she. "If he trusts to his neighbors, he will have to wait a while yet for his harvest."

Next day, the owner came again, and found the sun hotter, the corn riper, and nothing done.

"There is not an hour to be lost," said he. "We cannot depend upon our neighbors; we must call in our relations." Turning to his son, he said, "Go, call your uncles and cousins; and see that they begin to-morrow."

The young Larks, in great fear, told their mother what the Farmer had said. "If that be all," said she, "do not be frightened, for the relations have harvest work of their own; but take notice of what you hear next time, and be sure to let me know."

She went abroad the next day, and the owner coming, as before, and finding the grain falling to the ground because it was over ripe, said to his son, "We must wait no longer for our neighbors and friends. Do you go to-night and hire some reapers, and we will set to work ourselves to-morrow."

When the young Larks told their mother this, —

" Then," said she, " it is time for us to be off; for when a man takes up his business himself, instead of leaving it to others, you may be sure that he means to set to work in earnest."

BEAUTY AND THE BEAST.

I.

BEAUTY AND HER SISTERS.

THERE was once a rich merchant who had six children, three sons and three daughters; he loved them more than he loved all his riches, so that he was always seeking to make them happy and wise.

The daughters were very pretty; but the youngest was more than pretty — she was beautiful. As every one called her Little Beauty when she was a child, and she became more lovely every year, the name grew up with her, so that she had no other than just — Beauty.

Now Beauty was as good as she was beautiful; but her elder sisters were ill-natured and jealous of her, and could not bear to hear her called Beauty. They were very proud, too, of their father's riches, and put on great airs.

They would not visit the daughters of other merchants, but were always following persons who had titles, Lady this and Duchess that. They laughed at Beauty, who lived quietly at home with their father.

The father was so rich that many great merchants wished to marry his daughters, but the two eldest always said that they could never think of marrying anybody below a duke, or at the least an earl. As for Beauty, she thanked her lovers for thinking so well of her, but as she was still very young, she wished to live a few years longer with her father.

Now it fell out that the merchant all at once lost his great wealth. Nothing was left but one small house in the country, and there the poor man told his children they must now go, and earn their daily bread.

The two eldest daughters said they need not go, for they had plenty of lovers who would be glad enough to marry them, even though they had lost their fortune. But they were wrong, for their lovers would not look at them now, and jeered at them in their trouble, because they had been so proud before.

Yet every one felt sorry for Beauty. Several gentlemen who loved her begged her still to let them marry her, though she had not a penny. Beauty refused, and said she could not leave her father now that trouble had come upon him.

So the family went to live in the small house in the country. There the merchant and his three sons ploughed and sowed the fields, and worked hard all day. Beauty rose at four o'clock every morning, put the house in order, and got breakfast for the whole family. It was very hard at first, for no one helped her; but every day it grew easier to work, and Beauty grew stronger and rosier. When her work was done, she could read or play on her harp, or sit at her spinning-wheel, singing as she spun.

As for her two sisters, they were idle and unhappy, and became quite helpless. They never got up till ten o'clock, and then they spent the day moping and fretting, because they no longer had fine clothes to wear, and could not go to fine parties to be seen. They jeered at Beauty, and said that she was nothing but a servant-girl after all, to like that kind of living; but Beauty did not mind them, and lived on cheerfully.

They had been in the country a year, when one morning the merchant had a letter. It brought the news that a ship laden with rich goods belonging to him had not been lost after all, and had just come into port. The two sisters were half wild with joy, for now they could soon leave the farm-house, and go back to the gay city.

When their father was about to go to the

port to settle his business there, they begged him to bring back all manner of fine things for them.

Then the merchant asked Beauty : —

" And what shall I bring you Beauty ? " for Beauty had yet asked nothing.

" Why, since you ask me, dear father, I should like you to bring me a rose, for none grow in these parts." Now Beauty did not care so very much for a rose, but she did not like to seem to blame her sisters, or to appear better than they, by saying that she did not wish for anything.

The good man set off ; but all was not as he had hoped. The ship had come in, but there was a dispute about the cargo. He went to law, and it ended in his turning back poorer than when he left his home.

II.

THE BEAST AT HOME.

HE set out to return to the farm-house. When he was within thirty miles of home, he came to a large wood through which he must pass. The snow began to fall, and covered the path. The night closed in, and it grew so dark and so cold that the poor man gave himself up for lost. He could not see the way, and he was faint with cold and hunger.

All at once, he saw a light at the end of a long avenue of trees. He turned into the avenue, and rode until he came to the end of it. There he found a great palace; the windows were all lighted, and the door stood open, but he saw not a soul.

The door of the stable was also open, and his horse walked in. A crib full of hay and oats was there, and the tired beast fell to eating heartily. The merchant left his horse in the stall and entered the palace. He saw nobody and heard nobody, but a fire was burning on the hearth, and a table was spread with choice food, and set for one person. He was wet to the skin, and went to the fire to dry himself, saying : —

" I hope the master of the house or his servants will not blame me for this. No doubt some one will soon come."

He waited, but no one came. The clock struck eleven. Then, faint for want of food, he went to the table and ate some meat, yet all the time in a great fright. But when he was no longer hungry, he began to pluck up courage, and to look about him.

The clock struck twelve. He left the hall, and passed through one room after another until he came to one where there was a bed. It was made ready, and, since he was very tired, he lay down and slept soundly.

The merchant did not wake' until ten o'clock the next morning. He had placed his clothes on a chair by the side of the bed. They had been nearly ruined by the storm, and were besides old and worn. Now he saw a wholly new suit in their place.

He began to think he must be in the palace of some fairy, and he was sure of it when he looked out of the window. The snow had gone, and a lovely garden lay before him, full of flowers. He dressed and went back to the hall. A table was spread for breakfast, and he at once sat down to it. Then he went to get his horse. On the way he passed some roses. He remembered Beauty, and plucked a rose to take home with him.

As soon as he had done this, he heard a frightful roar, and saw a dreadful Beast coming toward him. He was so frightened that he nearly fell down. The Beast cried out in a loud voice : —

" Ungrateful man ! I saved your life by letting you come into my palace. I gave you food to eat and a bed to rest in, and now you steal my roses, which I love beyond everything. You shall pay for this with your life ! " The poor man threw himself on his knees before the Beast, saying : —

" Forgive me, my lord. I did not know I was doing wrong. I only wanted to pluck a rose for one of my daughters. She asked me to bring one home to her. I pray you, do not kill me, my lord."

"I am not a lord. I am a Beast. I hate soft words, and you will not catch me by any of your fine speeches. You say you have daughters. Well, I will forgive you, if one of them will come and die in your stead. But promise that, if they refuse, you will come back in three months."

The merchant did not mean in the least to let one of his daughters die for him. But he wished to see his children once more before he died, so he promised to return if one of his daughters would not die for him. The Beast then told him to go back to the room where he had slept. There he would find a chest. He might fill it with anything he found in the palace, and it would be sent after him.

III.

BEAUTY GOES TO THE BEAST.

THE merchant did as he was bid. The floor of the room was covered with gold, and he filled the chest. If he must die, he would at least provide for his children. Then he took his horse and rode out of the wood, and came at last to his home. He held the rose in his hand, and

as the daughters came out to meet him, he gave
it to the youngest, saying : —

"Take it, Beauty. You little know what it
has cost your poor father ; " and then he told all
that had happened since he left home.

The two eldest daughters began to cry aloud,
and to blame Beauty. Why did she ask for
roses? Why did she not ask for dresses, as
they did; then all would have gone well. Now
the hard-hearted thing, they said, did not shed a
tear. Beauty replied quietly that it was of little
use to weep. She meant to go and die in her
father's stead.

"No, no!" cried the three brothers. "We
will go and seek this Beast, and either he or we
must die!"

"It is all in vain," said the father. "You do
not know the Beast. He is more mighty than
you can think. No! you must stay and care for
your sisters. At the end of three months I shall
go back and die." The merchant then went to
his room, and there he found the chest of gold.

He was greatly amazed. He had forgotten
the promise of the Beast. But he said nothing
about the chest to his daughters. He was sure
they would tease him to go back to town to live.

Beauty said little, but when the three months
were over, she made ready to go with her father.
The brothers and sisters bade them good-by,

and wept over Beauty. The brothers wept real tears, but the sisters rubbed their eyes with onions, so as to make tears; they did not really care.

The horse took the right road, as if he knew the way, and when he came to the palace, he went at once to the stable. The merchant and Beauty entered the palace. They found the table spread for two persons, and they sat down to it.

After supper there was a great roar as before, and the Beast entered. Beauty trembled, and the Beast turned to her and said : —

"Did you come of your own self?"

"Yes," said Beauty, still trembling.

"Then I thank you. But you, sir," and he turned to the father, "get you gone to-morrow, and never let me see your face again. Good-night, Beauty."

"Good-night, Beast," she replied, and Beast walked off. The merchant begged and begged his daughter to leave him, and to go back to her home. But she was firm, and when the morning came, she made him leave her.

"Surely," he thought, "Beast will not hurt Beauty."

Beauty wept, but she was a brave girl, and soon she dried her eyes, and began to walk through the palace. She came to a door and

over it was written BEAUTY'S ROOM. She
opened the door, and found herself in a fine
chamber, with books, music and a harp, and
many beautiful things.

"It cannot be that I have only a day to live,"
she said, "for why should all this be done for
me?" She opened a book and saw written in
letters of gold: *Your wishes and commands
shall be obeyed. You are here the queen over
everything.*

"Alas!" she thought, "I wish most of all I
could see my father and know what he is doing."
Just then her eyes fell on a large looking-glass,
and in it she saw her father just reaching home.
Her sisters came out to meet him. They tried
to look sad, but it was plain that they were not
sorry to see him come home alone.

The sight in the glass was only for a moment;
then it faded, and Beauty turned away and in
her mind thanked Beast for what he had done.

At noon she found dinner ready for her, and
sweet music sounded as she ate. But she saw
nobody. At night Beast came and asked leave
to sup with her. Of course she could not say
no, but she sat in a fright all through supper.
He did not speak for some time. Then he
said : —

"Beauty, do you think me very ugly?"

"Yes, Beast; I cannot tell a lie. But I think

you are very good." Nothing more was said, and Beauty was beginning to be rid of her fear, when all at once he asked : —

"Beauty, will you marry me?" Beauty was in a fright again, but she answered : —

"No, Beast." He gave a great sigh which shook the house. Then he got up from the table and said : —

"Good - night, Beauty," and went away. Beauty was glad he had gone, but she could not help pitying him.

IV.

THE CHARM IS BROKEN.

BEAUTY lived in this way three months. The Beast came to supper every night. He did not grow less ugly, but Beauty did not mind his ugliness so much, for she saw how kind he really was. But there was one sore trouble. Every night the Beast was sure to ask : —

"Will you marry me, Beauty?" and Beauty always answered : —

"No, Beast."

But one night he begged her at least never to leave him. Now it chanced on that very day Beauty had looked in her glass. There she saw her father sick with grief, for he thought his

child was dead.   Her sisters were married.   Her
brothers were soldiers.   So she told all this to
the Beast, and wept and said she should die if
she could not see her father once more.

"Do not refuse to let me go!" she begged.

"No," said the Beast.   "I will not refuse you.
I would much rather your poor Beast should die
of grief for your absence.   So you may go."

"Oh, thank you dear Beast," said Beauty,
"and I will surely come back in a week."

"When you wish to come back, Beauty, lay
your ring on the table before you go to bed,
and you will find yourself here when you wake.
Good-night, Beauty."

"Good-night, Beast."

The next morning Beauty woke to find herself
at the farm-house.   Her father was so glad to
see her once more, and to know she was alive
and well, that his sickness left him at once.   He
sent for her sisters, who came and brought their
husbands.

These husbands were not much to be praised.
One was so vain that he looked at himself, and
seldom looked at his wife.   The other had a sharp
tongue, and liked to use it on other people, and
most of all on his own wife.   So the sisters were
no happier than they had been.

But they were still jealous of Beauty, and
they laid a plan for her hurt.   They thought if

they could keep her at home after the week was over, the Beast would be so angry, he would soon make an end of her. So, at the end of the week, they made a great ado, and begged her to stay just a little longer. Beauty could not help being glad to have her sisters want her. She said she would stay one week more; but she was not quite easy in her mind.

On the night of the tenth day the sisters gave her a feast, in order to make her forget the Beast. But at night Beauty dreamed she saw poor Beast lying half dead on the grass in the palace garden. She woke in tears, and at once laid her ring on the table, and then went to sleep again.

When she awoke, she was once more in her room at the palace. All day she wished for supper time to come. Then she would see Beast again. But supper time came, and no Beast was at the table. Nine o'clock struck, and still Beast did not come.

Beauty flew into the garden. She went to the spot she had dreamed of, and there lay poor Beast on the grass. She felt his heart beat. He was still alive. She ran for some water and threw it on his face. The Beast opened his eyes and said in a faint voice: —

" You forgot your promise. I could not live without you, and I meant to starve to death. Now you have come, and I shall die happy."

"No! you shall not die, dear Beast," cried Beauty. "You shall live to be my husband, for now I feel I really love you."

At these words the whole palace was ablaze with light. Music sounded, and there was a stir all about. There was no Beast, but in his place a very handsome prince was at Beauty's feet.

"You have broken the charm that held me," he said.

"But where is my poor Beast?" asked Beauty, weeping. "I want my dear Beast."

"I was the Beast," said the Prince. "A wicked fairy had power to make me live in that ugly form, till some good and beautiful maid should be found, so good as to love me in spite of my ugliness."

Beauty was amazed, but she took the Prince's hand and they went into the palace. The people of the country were full of joy. They had mourned for their Prince, and now he had suddenly come back again, and with him was a beautiful princess. So Beauty and the Beast, who was no longer a Beast, reigned happily in the kingdom.

THE LION IN LOVE.

A LION once fell in love with a Woodman's daughter, and wished to marry her. So he went to the father, and begged him to give him the maid.

The Woodman said he could not think of marrying his daughter to a Lion. At that the Lion began to roar terribly. The Woodman was in great fright, but thought of a way out of the danger.

"Lion," said he, "I will give you my daughter, if you will first have your nails and your teeth drawn; for it is these that frighten her."

The Lion was so madly in love that he went at once and had his nails and his teeth drawn; but now, when he came back for the maid, the Woodman had no more fear of him, and drove him away with jeers.

THE TRAVELER AND THE VIPER.

A MAN, going along the road in winter, saw a Viper stiff with cold; he had pity on him, and took him up, and placed him in his bosom to warm him back into life.

Now the Viper, as long as he was cold, lay quiet; but as soon as he was well warmed, he drove his fangs into the man's breast.

As the man lay dying, he said : —

" I suffer justly ; for why should I have taken care of the dying Viper, when I ought to have killed him, if he had been in the best of health?"

THE WOLF AND THE LAMB.

A Wolf saw a Lamb drinking at a brook, and set about finding some good reason for catching him. So he went to a place a little higher up the brook, and called out : —

" How dare you muddle the water that I am drinking ?"

"How can I," said the Lamb, humbly, "when I drink with the tips of my lips only? And, besides, the water runs from you to me, not from me to you."

" Well, you called my father names a year ago," said the Wolf, readily finding another reason.

" I was not born a year ago," said the poor Lamb.

" You may make ever so good excuses," said the Wolf, finally ; "I shall eat you all the same."

This fable teaches that, when one has made up his mind to do wrong, he is not stopped by the best of reasons.

THE TRAVELERS AND THE AXE.

Two men were traveling along the same road, when one of them found an axe. At that the other, who had not found it, begged him not to say " I found the axe," but " We found the axe."

By and by the people who had lost the axe met them, and the one who had found it was set upon by them. As he tried to escape, he cried out : " We are undone ! "

But his fellow-traveler answered : —

" Do not say ' We are undone,' but ' I am undone ; ' for when you found the axe, you said ' I found the axe,' not ' We found the axe.' "

Those who do not share their good fortune with others will find none to share their ill fortune.

THE TORTOISE AND THE EAGLE.

A Tortoise, seeing an Eagle in flight, wanted much to fly like him. So she asked him if he would not teach her to fly.

He told her that it was impossible; that Tortoises could not fly. All the more did she urge him, so at last the Eagle seized her in his claws, bore her to a great height, and then, letting her go, bade her fly.

She fell like a stone to the earth, and the blow knocked the breath out of her body.

This fable teaches that men who are envious, and refuse to take the advice of those who know more than themselves, are apt to get into trouble.

THE WHITE CAT.

I.

THE PALACE OF THE WHITE CAT.

A KING had three sons, handsome, brave, and generous. Some persons about the court, however, made him believe that these sons of his were eager to have him die or leave the throne, because they each wanted to be king. This was not at all true, but the King believed it, and made a plan to get them out of the way. He sent for them and said : —

"My dear sons, you must see that I am growing old, and cannot attend to state affairs as I once used to. It is right that I should make one of you king in my stead; but first I should like something to amuse me when I am no longer king. I think I should like best a little dog. Now, the one of you who brings me the most perfect little dog shall be king in my stead."

The princes were much surprised at the fancy of their father to have a little dog, but they all agreed to do as he had asked. They bade him good-by, and promised to come back in a year. They went off together to an old palace three miles away. There they had something to eat, and then set off on separate roads. But they agreed to meet again at the palace at the end of the year.

Now, we will see what happened to the youngest of the three brothers. He went from town to town looking for handsome dogs. He bought one, and then, when he found a handsomer dog, he bought that and gave the other away. He could not keep all the dogs. Twenty servants would not have been enough to carry them about, and take care of them. He kept only the handsomest one.

At last he found himself in a wood. Night came on, and it began to rain. There were thunder and lightning, and he lost his way. He groped about and saw a light in the distance. He went toward it, and soon was in front of a fine palace.

The door to the palace was of gold, studded with sapphires, and these shone with a bright light. This was the light the Prince had seen. The walls of the palace were of fine china, and there were wonderful paintings upon them.

These paintings showed the adventures of all the fairies from the beginning of the world.

The Prince saw a deer's foot hanging by the side of the door. It was hung at the end of a chain of diamonds, and was plainly a bell-pull. He was greatly astonished, for he saw no one, and he wondered that thieves had not long ago stolen the diamonds and the sapphires.

He pulled the deer's foot and heard a bell ring. Soon the golden door opened. He saw nobody, but he saw twelve Hands in the air, each holding a torch. He looked and did not know what to do. Then he felt himself gently pushed from behind, so he walked on into the palace. There he heard a voice singing : —

> " Welcome Prince, no danger fear,
> Mirth and love attend you here."

The Hands with the torches led him through one door after another, into one room after another. Each room was more splendid than the last. Finally the Hands drew a chair near a fire, and beckoned him to sit down.

The Hands he saw were white and fair. They took away his wet clothes, and brought him new fine linen, and a warm wrapper in which he sat before the fire. Then they placed before him a glass upon a stand, and began to comb and brush his hair gently. They brought a bowl with perfumed water in it, and washed his face and hands.

Now the Prince was fresh and warm, and the Hands gave him a princely suit of clothes. When he was dressed, they led him out of the chamber to a grand hall. Here a table was set with rich and dainty food. Two plates were on the table, and the Prince wondered who was to eat with him.

II.

A YEAR OF SPORT.

JUST then he looked up and saw a small figure coming toward him. It was covered with a long black veil, and was not more than a foot high. On each side walked a cat dressed in black, and behind came a great number of cats, some carrying cages full of rats, and others mouse-traps filled with mice.

The Prince did not know what to think. The little figure drew near, and drew aside her veil. It was a cat, a beautiful White Cat, but looking sad and gentle. She said to the Prince : —

"You are welcome, Prince. It makes me glad to have you come."

"Madam," said the Prince, "I thank you for all your goodness to me. I cannot help thinking you must be a wonderful being, to have this beautiful palace, to be able to speak, and yet — to be a cat!"

"That is true," said the Cat, "but I do not like to talk, and I do not like to hear fine things said to me. Let us sit down to supper."

The Hands then placed some dishes on the table, in front of the Prince and the White Cat. The Prince had a pie made of young pigeons, but the White Cat had one made of fat mice. The Prince at first did not like to touch his food. He was not quite sure what it was, but the White Cat told him not to be afraid. The dishes before him had no bit of rat or mouse in them.

When supper was over, the Prince noticed that the White Cat carried a little picture hung by a cord upon one of her feet. He asked to look at it. It was a portrait of a young man. To his great surprise, it was his own likeness.

He did not ask the White Cat to explain this, for she had a look which forbade him. They talked together about many things, and then the White Cat bade the Prince good-night. The Hands, with torches, led him to his chamber, and there he slept.

He was waked in the morning by a noise outside. He got up, and the Hands brought him a handsome hunting-jacket. The noise kept on, and he looked out of the window. There he saw more than five hundred cats in the open space before the palace. They were making ready for a hunt.

The White Cat soon came and asked him to join their sport, and he was given a wooden-horse to ride on. The White Cat mounted a monkey. She wore a dragoon's cap, which made her look very bold and fierce.

The horns sounded, and away they went. The cats ran faster than the hares and rabbits, and when they caught any they brought them to the Prince and the White Cat. They chased birds as well as rabbits. Up the trees they went, and the White Cat on the monkey climbed more quickly than any, and mounted the highest trees, to the eagle's nest.

When the chase was over, they all went back to the palace. The White Cat sat down at the table with the Prince, and they had a fine supper. Again the Hands led the Prince to his chamber, and he slept soundly.

So it went on day after day. Every day there was some new pleasure, and the White Cat was so gentle, so sweet, and so thoughtful, that the Prince could not bear to think of leaving the palace.

"How can I go away from you?" he cried one day. "Can you not make me a cat to live here always? or, can you not make yourself a lady?" But the White Cat only smiled, and made no answer.

At last a year had almost gone. The White

Cat knew what day the Prince must return to his father, and told him that he had but three days left.

"Alas!" said the Prince. "What shall I do? I have not yet found a dog small enough."

"Never fear," said the White Cat. "I will see that you have a dog, and I will also give you a wooden-horse, so that you can ride home in a few hours."

When the day came, the White Cat gave the Prince an acorn, and told him to put it close to his ear. He did so, and could hear a little dog barking inside the acorn. He was delighted, and thanked the White Cat a thousand times.

III.

THE LITTLE DOG AND THE CAMBRIC.

The Prince mounted his wooden horse, and soon was at the place where he was to meet his brothers. The two eldest told their stories. The youngest kept silence, and showed only a cheap cur. The brothers trod on each other's toes under the table, as much as to say, "We have nothing to fear from this dog."

The next day they all went to the palace. The dogs of the two elder brothers were brought in on soft rugs; they were wrapped

about in silk quilts, and it was hard to see anything of them. However, the King looked at
each, and could not make up his mind which
was the smaller and prettier. So the two
princes began to quarrel.

At this the youngest son came forward. Nobody had looked at his cur, but now he showed
them his acorn. He broke the shell, and out
jumped a little dog. He held his finger ring,
and the dog leaped through it. There was no
doubt now who had the smallest and prettiest
dog.

The King could not possibly find any fault
with the dog, but he could not bear to give up
his crown yet. So he thanked his sons for their
trouble, and asked them to try once more. He
wished them to be gone a year, and at the end
of that time to bring him a fine piece of cambric. It must be fine enough to be drawn
through the eye of a small needle.

The three princes thought this very hard, but
they set off as before. The two eldest took dif-
ferent roads. The youngest mounted his wooden-
horse, and quickly came to the palace of the
White Cat. There he was received with great
joy. The Hands helped him to dismount, and
the table was spread before him. The best
food was given him, and the White Cat sat op-
posite. He told her what a hard task his father
had set.

"Do not be troubled," she said. "I have cats in my palace who can make just such cambric. So be at ease and enjoy yourself."

The Prince knew how to enjoy himself. He talked with the White Cat about all sorts of things, and they hunted together. And when he was alone, why, he could think about the White Cat, and what she said last. Oh yes, he knew how to enjoy himself.

Thus another year went by. At the end of the year the White Cat said to the Prince: —

" This time you must go in state."

Then he saw in the yard a splendid carriage, covered with gold and diamonds. Twelve horses as white as snow were harnessed to it, and a troop of horsemen was ready to ride behind and by the side of the carriage. The White Cat bade the Prince good-by, and gave him a walnut.

" In this nut," she said, " is the cambric. But you must not open the nut till you come before the King."

Away went the horses, and carried the Prince in a twinkling to the King's palace. His two brothers were already there. They all went into the King's presence, and the eldest brought out his piece of cambric. No one had ever seen anything so fine. The King took the needle. The tip end of the cambric went through the eye, but the piece could not be pulled further.

The second son tried, but his piece failed also. Then the youngest Prince came forward with an elegant box, covered with jewels. He opened the box and took out the walnut. He smiled, and looked about, and cracked the shell. Then he looked sober. There was no cambric here, only a filbert.

However, he cracked the shell of the filbert. Out came a cherry-stone. He looked more serious still. The brothers and the lords of the court began to laugh. What could be more silly than this Prince with his cherry-stone!

The Prince now cracked the cherry-stone, and took out the kernel. He split it, and found a grain of wheat; he opened the grain of wheat, and there was a grain of millet-seed. All the court was now laughing. The Prince grew red in the face and muttered : —

" O White Cat, White Cat, you have deceived me."

When he said this he felt a scratch on his arm. He saw nothing, but it was just as if a cat scratched him. That brought him to his senses. He opened the millet-seed very carefully, and drew forth a piece of cambric. It was four hundred yards long, and was so fine that it was easily drawn through the eye of the needle.

The King could ask nothing more. But he

was not ready to give up his crown, so he said to his sons : —

"You have done nobly. Now one of you must be king. But it will not do for one to be king without a queen. So go away and find the most beautiful woman in the world. At the end of the year come back. The one who brings the most beautiful woman shall marry her and have my kingdom."

IV.

THE WHITE CAT HAS HER HEAD CUT OFF.

THE three brothers set off again on their travels, and the youngest rode straight to the palace of the White Cat. He could not bear to speak or think of his errand. He was so happy, however, with the White Cat that he quite forgot everything for another year. At the end of that time, the White Cat herself reminded him what he had to do.

"You must now go back to your father, but you shall take with you a beautiful princess. Cut off my head and my tail, and throw them into the fire."

"I!" said the Prince. "I cut off your head and tail! How can I, when I love you so?"

"You must. That is the way to prove your love. If you love me, do as I bid you."

The Prince looked at the White Cat. Her eyes said the same thing to him. He took his sword, and did as she bade him. No sooner had he done this than the White Cat was gone, and a beautiful princess stood before him. At the same moment the room was full of maids and gentlemen. All the cats were gone. The Prince was astonished. The beautiful princess sent away all the people, and then told the story of her life to the Prince.

V.

THE WHITE CAT'S STORY.

"Do not think I have always been a cat. My father was a king, and had six kingdoms. He loved my mother dearly, and let her do just as she wished. She liked best to travel and to see new sights. One day she heard of a distant country where the fairies had a garden, and in this garden was the most delicious fruit ever eaten.

"She wished at once to taste this fruit, and so she set off for the country. She came to a noble palace and knocked at the gate. No one came out. She waited. No one appeared anywhere in sight. But over the garden wall she saw the fruit.

"My mother bade her servants pitch her tent close by the gate. There she stayed six weeks. Yet she saw no one go in or out. She was so vexed and so disappointed that at the end of six weeks she fell sick.

"One night, when she was almost dead, she opened her eyes and saw an old woman, small and ugly. It was one of the fairies who owned the garden. This old woman was sitting in a chair by the bed, and spoke to my mother.

"'Why do you come here for our fruit?' she asked. 'My sisters and I do not like it at all. We did not mean you should have any. But now you are very ill, and we do not want you to die here, you may have all you want, if you will give us what we ask and then go away.'

"'Oh,' said my mother, 'I will give you everything I have, to the half of my kingdom, if you will only give me the fruit.'

"'Very well. You will have a child. When the child is born, give her to us. We will take care of her, and she shall be a beautiful princess.'

"'That is pretty hard,' said my mother, 'but I must have the fruit, or I shall die. So the child shall be yours.'

"Then my mother rose and dressed, and went into the garden. Here she ate her fill. Besides, she ordered four thousand mules to be loaded with the fruit, for it was of a kind that would never spoil. Thus she traveled back to my father. He was overjoyed to see her, and she said nothing of the promise she had given.

" By and by, however, she grew sad, and my father asked her what troubled her. Then she told him the whole story. At first he was greatly troubled, but he began to think how he should prevent the fairies from getting his child.

" As soon as I was born he had me taken to the top of a high tower. There were twenty flights of stairs leading up to the room in which I was placed. A door was at the foot of each flight, and was locked, and my father kept the key. He did not mean that any one should get at me.

" When the fairies heard of this, they were very angry. They sent forth a great dragon, and the dragon breathed forth fire, and burnt up the grass and trees. It was very fierce, too, and killed men, women, and children. So my father was filled with dismay, and sent word that the fairies should have me."

VI.

THE WHITE CAT'S STORY ENDED.

" I was placed in a cradle of mother-of-pearl, and carried to the palace by the garden, where my mother had eaten the fruit. The dragon at once disappeared, and all went well in my father's kingdom.

" The fairies gave me a room in a tower, and I had everything I could ask. Here I grew up. I knew nothing of my father or mother. The fairies came to see me, but they rode the dragon, and flew in at the window. You must know, there was no door to the tower. There were windows, high up from the ground, and there was a garden upon the top of the tower.

" The fairies were very kind to me, and all went well. I played in the garden on the tower, and I had my birds and flowers. But one day I was sitting at one of the windows talking with my parrot, when I saw a fine-looking man below. He stood listening to the parrot and me.

" I never had seen a man except in pictures, and I was very glad to see this one. We spoke to each other through the window, and so it went on day after day. At last I thought I could not bear to live alone in the tower, and I planned to escape.

" I begged the fairies to bring me some cord and needles, to make a net with. There were birds flying about, and if I had a net I could catch one. They gave me these things, and I made a ladder which reached from my window to the ground.

" I meant to climb down the ladder, but before I could do so my lover had climbed up. He leaped in at my window. At first I was frightened, but then I was glad to have him with me. He gave me a picture of himself, but while we were talking the fairy Violent flew in at the window on the back of the dragon. She was in a great rage, and bade the dragon at once devour my lover.

" I tried to cast myself into the mouth of the dragon, for I no longer cared to live. But the fairy held me back, and said she had another punishment for me. She touched me with her wand, and I became at once a White Cat.

" She brought me to this palace, and gave me a troop of cats to wait on me. They were lords and ladies who had been turned into cats. The Hands were the hands of servants who could not be seen. Here I was to stay a cat until a prince should come who looked exactly like my lover, and who should cut off my head and my tail.

" My Prince, look at this picture. It is your exact image. You have saved me from the fairies, and I love you with all my heart."

The Prince was overjoyed. He made haste to set out for his father's palace with the beautiful princess. Again the brothers stood before the King, each with a beautiful princess. The King was now at his wit's end, but the princess, who had lately been a White Cat, came forward and said : —

" O King, it is a thousand pities that you should give up your kingdom. You are not old. You are very wise, and ought to reign many years. I have six kingdoms. Let me give one to each of your two eldest sons. Then the youngest son and I will still have four kingdoms. More than all, you will not have to decide which of us three princesses is the most beautiful."

Everybody set up a shout. The three weddings took place at once, and the kingdoms were divided between the princes.

THE JACKDAW AND THE DOVES.

A JACKDAW once looked into a dove-cote, and saw the Doves well fed and cared for; so he went away and daubed himself white, and then went back to make himself one of them. As long as he kept quiet they let him stay, thinking he was a Dove; but as soon as he opened his mouth to speak or sing, they found

out who he was, and drove him out of the dove-
cote.

He, poor fellow, now went back to the Jack-
daws, but they did not know him on account of
his white coat, and would not let him join them.

And so, for wanting to get into two compa-
nies, he missed both.

This fable teaches that it is best for us to be
content with our own kind, showing that the
greedy not only miss what they seek, but often
lose what they have.

THE HARES AND THE FROGS.

THE HARES once got together, and agreed
that they led a very hard life; that they were
always in a scare. Men chased them, and dogs,
and eagles; they had no peace, and it was better to die once for all than to live in a constant
fright.

So they all started for a pond, to throw themselves off a rock into the water and end their
wretched life.

Now some Frogs were sitting around the
edge of the pond, and heard the noise made by
the Hares as they came running. They were
so frightened that they all jumped at once into
the water.

"Hold on!" cried one of the Hares to his

fellows. " Do nothing rash. Do you not see that there are others more scared than we? "

THE FOUR BULLS AND THE LION.

FOUR BULLS once agreed to live together, and they fed in the same pasture. Now the Lion saw them afar off, and wanted to hunt them, but he knew that he could not so long as they held together.

So he managed to set them quarreling with each other, and when that happened, they separated, and he easily mastered them one at a time.

THE COUNTRY MAID AND HER MILK-PAIL.

A COUNTRY MAID was walking slowly along with a pail of milk upon her head, and thinking thus : —

" The money for which I shall sell this milk will buy me three hundred eggs. These eggs, allowing for what may prove addled, will produce at least two hundred and fifty chickens. The chickens will be fit to carry to market about Christmas, when poultry always brings a good price, so that by May-day I shall have money enough to buy a new gown. Let me see — green suits me ; yes, it shall be green. In this dress I will go to the fair, where all the young fellows will want me for a partner, but I shall refuse every one of them." By this time she was so full of her fancy that she tossed her head proudly, when over went the pail, which she had entirely forgotten, and all the milk was spilled on the ground.

Moral. Don't count your chickens before they are hatched.

THE LION, THE ASS, AND THE FOX.

THE Lion, the Ass, and the Fox made a bargain to hunt together. Now, when they had caught a good supply of game, they came to eat it, and the Lion bade the Ass divide the spoils. So the Ass divided it into three equal parts, and called on each to choose his portion. At that the Lion fell into a rage, and made his supper off the Ass.

Then the Lion told the Fox to divide it, and he put almost all the game into one great heap for the Lion, and saved only a small bit for himself. Then the Lion said: "My good fellow, who taught you to divide so well?" And the Fox said: "That dead Ass there."

THE FISHERMAN AND HIS WIFE.

I.

THE FIRST WISH.

ONCE upon a time there was a Fisherman who lived with his wife in a hut in a ditch, near the sea. The Fisherman used to go out all day long to catch fish. One day, as he sat on the shore with his rod, he felt his line pulled; he drew it in, and at the end was a great Fish. The Fish said to him : —

"Pray let me live; I am not a real Fish. I am an enchanted Prince ; put me into the water again and let me go."

"Oh," said the Fisherman, "you need not make so many words about the matter. I wish to have nothing to do with a Fish that can talk. So swim away as fast as ou please."

He put him back into the water; the Fish darted straight down to the bottom, and left a long streak of blood behind him. When the Fisherman went home to his wife in the ditch, he told her of the Fish.

"Did you not ask it for anything ? " said the wife.

" No," said the Fisherman. " What should I ask for ? "

" Ah ! " said the wife, " we live meanly here

in this poor ditch. Go back and tell the Fish we want a little cottage."

The Fisherman did not much like to do this; but he went to the sea, and looked out. The water was yellow and green. He stood on the edge, and cried : —

> "O man of the sea !
> Come, listen to me,
> For Alice my wife,
> The plague of my life,
> Hath sent me to beg a boon of thee."

At that the Fish swam to him, and said : —
" Well, what does she want ? "

" Ah ! " said the Fisherman, " my wife says that when I had caught you, I ought to have asked you for something, before I let you go again. She does not like to live in the ditch ; she wants a little cottage."

" Go home, then," said the Fish. " She is in the cottage already." So the Fisherman went home, and saw his wife at the door of a cottage.

" Come in, come in," said she; " is not this much better than the ditch ? " And there were a parlor and a chamber and a kitchen ; behind the cottage was a little garden, with all sorts of flowers and fruits, and a yard full of ducks and chickens.

" Ah ! " said the Fisherman, " how happily we shall live now."

" At least we can try," answered his wife.

II.

THE SECOND WISH.

ALL went well for a week or two, and then Dame Alice said : —

"Husband, there is not room enough in this cottage; the garden and the yard are both too small. I should like a large stone castle to live in. So go to the Fish, and tell him to give us a castle."

"Wife," said the Fisherman, "I do not like to ask again ; I fear he will be angry ; let us be content with the cottage."

"Nonsense! he will give you what you ask. Go along and try."

The Fisherman went, but his heart was heavy.

He came to the sea, and the water was gray and gloomy, but it was calm. He stood on the edge and cried again : —

"O man of the sea !
Come, listen to me,
For Alice my wife,
The plague of my life,
Hath sent me to beg a boon of thee ! "

"Well, what does she want now?" asked the Fish.

"Ah!" said the Fisherman, "my wife wants to live in a stone castle."

"Go home then, she is standing at the door of it already." Away went the Fisherman, and found his wife standing before a great castle.

"See," said she, "is not this grand?" With that they both went into the castle, and found men and maids waiting to serve them. The rooms were full of golden chairs and tables; behind the castle was a garden, and a wood half a mile long, full of hares and deer; sheep and goats were in the field, and in the yard were stables and cow-houses.

"Well!" said the Fisherman, "now we will live contented and happy here the rest of our lives."

"Perhaps we may," replied his wife; "but let us sleep over it, and see how it is in the morning." So they went to bed.

III.

THE THIRD WISH.

When dame Alice awoke the next day, she jogged the Fisherman with her elbow and cried:

"Husband, get up, bestir yourself, for we must be king of all the land."

"Wife, wife," said the Fisherman, "why should we wish to be king? I will not be king."

"Then I will," said Alice.

" But wife, how can you be king? the Fish cannot make you a king."

" Husband," she said, " say no more, but go, ask the Fish. I will be king." So the Fisherman went once more to the sea, grieving much over his wife. The waves were a dark gray and were covered with foam. He stood on the edge, and cried again : —

> "O man of the sea !
> Come, listen to me,
> For Alice my wife,
> The plague of my life,
> Hath sent me to beg a boon of thee."

" Well, what does she want now ? " asked the Fish.

" Alas," said the Fisherman, " my wife wants to be king."

" Go home," said the Fish ; " she is king already."

Then the Fisherman went home. As he came close to the palace, he saw a troop of soldiers, and heard the sound of drums and trumpets ; when he went in, he saw his wife on a high throne ; she had a gold crown on her head ; and on each side of her stood six beautiful maids, each a head taller than the other.

" Well, wife," said the Fisherman, " are you king ? "

" Yes," said she, " I am king." And when he had looked at her a long time, he said : —

" Ah, wife ! what a fine thing it is to be king ! now we shall never have anything more to wish for."

IV.

THE FOURTH WISH.

" I DON'T know how that may be," said Alice. " Never is a long time. I am king 't is true; but I begin to be tired of it, and I think I should like to be emperor."

" Alas, wife ! why should you wish to be emperor ? " asked the Fisherman.

" Husband," said she, "go to the Fish. I say I will be emperor."

" Ah, wife ! the Fish cannot make you emperor, and I do not like to ask such a thing."

" I am king," said Alice, " and you are my slave. Go at once."

So the Fisherman must needs go ; but he said to himself, as he went : —

" This will come to no good ; it is too much to ask; the Fish will be tired at last, and then we shall repent of what we have done." He came to the sea ; the water was black, and a great whirlwind blew over it ; but he went to the edge of the shore, and cried : —

> " O man of the sea !
> Come, listen to me,
> For Alice my wife,
> The plague of my life,
> Hath sent me to beg a boon of thee."

" Well, what does she want now? " asked the
Fish.

" Ah," said he, " she wants to be emperor."

" Go home," said the Fish, " she is emperor."

So he went home again ; as he drew near, he
saw his wife sitting on a very lofty throne,
made of solid gold ; she had a gold crown on
her head, full two yards high, and on each side
of her stood her guards in a row, each smaller
than the other, from the tallest giant down to a
wee dwarf, no bigger than her finger. Before
her stood princes, and dukes, and earls ; and the
Fisherman went up to her, and said : —

" Wife, are you emperor ? "

" Yes," said she, " I am emperor."

V.

THE FIFTH WISH.

" AH," said the man, as he gazed up at her,
" what a fine thing it is to be emperor ! "

" Husband," said she, " why should we stay at
being emperor ? I will be pope next."

" O wife ! " said he, " how can you be pope ?
There is but one pope at a time in the world."

" Husband," said she, " I will be pope this
very day."

" But," answered the husband, " the Fish cannot make you pope."

"What nonsense!" said she; "if he can make me an emperor, he can make me a pope. Go and try him."

So the Fisherman went. But when he came to the shore, the wind was raging and the sea was tossed up and down like boiling water; in the middle of the sky there was a little blue, but toward the south it was red, as if a dreadful storm was brewing. At this, the Fisherman was in terror, but he went to the edge of the shore, and said in a low voice: —

> "O man of the sea!
> Come, listen to me,
> For Alice my wife,
> The plague of my life,
> Hath sent me to beg a boon of thee."

"Well, what does she want now?" asked the Fish.

"Ah!" said the Fisherman, "she wants to be pope."

"Go home; she is pope."

Then the Fisherman went home and found his wife sitting on a throne that was two miles high; she had three great crowns on her head: — around her stood all the pomp and power of the church; and on each side were two rows of burning lights, of all sizes, the greatest as large as the tallest tower in the world, and the least no bigger than a small rush-light.

" Wife," said the Fisherman, as he looked at all this grandeur, " are you pope?"

" Yes," said she, " I am pope."

" Well, wife," replied he " it is a grand thing to be pope, and now you must be content, for you can be nothing greater."

" I will consider of that," said the wife.

VI.

THE FINAL WISH.

THEY went to bed, but dame Alice could not sleep all night, for thinking of what she should be next. At last morning came and the sun rose.

" Ha!" thought she, as she looked at it through the window, " cannot I prevent the sun rising?" At this she grew very angry, and she waked her husband, and said : —

" Husband, go to the Fish and tell him I want to be lord of the sun and moon."

The Fisherman was half asleep, but the thought so scared him that he started and fell out of bed.

" Alas, wife!" said he, " cannot you be content to be pope?"

" No," said she, " I am very uneasy, and cannot bear to see the sun and moon rise without my leave. Go at once to the Fish."

Then the man went, quaking with fear; as he drew near the shore, a great storm arose, so that the trees and the rocks shook, the sky became black, the lightning flashed, the thunder rolled. The sea was one mass of black waves with a white crown of foam; and the Fisherman whispered : —

> "O man of the sea !
> Come, listen to me,
> For Alice my wife,
> The plague of my life,
> Hath sent me to beg a boon of thee."

"What does she want ? "

"Ah ! " said the Fisherman, "she wants to be lord of the sun and moon."

"Go home," said the Fish, "to your ditch again." And there they live to this very day.

THE KID AND THE WOLF.

A KID stood on top of a house, and saw a Wolf go by below. He began to jeer at the Wolf, and to make all manner of fun of him.

"O ho ! " said the Wolf; "it is not you, it is the safe place where you are, that laughs at me."

This fable teaches that the place in which one is, or the time in which one acts, often gives one great boldness.

THE CAT, THE WEASEL, AND THE YOUNG RABBIT.

THERE was once a young Rabbit, a quiet, peace-loving Rabbit. He lived in a neat house, and made no trouble for any one. But one day he went to market to buy some parsley ; a Weasel came slyly by and saw the little house ; he slipped in and made himself at home. It was a good place to stay in, and there he meant to stay. By and by the Rabbit came home, and saw the Weasel at the window.

"Do you know that this is my house?" the Rabbit asked.

"Pooh, pooh!" said the Weasel, "what makes it yours?" You only dug in the ground a little, and came in here where the earth was gone. Do you think you own the earth?"

"The law gives it to me," said the Rabbit, "because I made it fit to live in. If you do not leave, I will call the police."

"The law, indeed!" said the Weasel; "and pray, what right has the law to give away land? But we will have no more words. We will lay the matter before the Cat, and leave it to him."

"Very well," said the young Rabbit, and they went to find the Cat, — an old, wise, and strong Cat.

"Come nearer, my children," said the Cat, as they both began to talk at the same time. "I am very deaf; nearer, for I wish to hear every word."

They came close to the Cat, each talking loudly. But as soon as the Cat had them within reach, he darted his claws out on each side, and held them both fast. First he made way with the young Rabbit, next with the Weasel; and then the house belonged to him.

THE WOMAN AND HER MAIDS.

A WOMAN, who was a busy housekeeper, was wont to wake her maids and set them at work by cock-crow. They thought this very hard, and said : —

" Come, let us kill the cock, for then the Mistress will not wake."

But when they had done this, they were worse off than before. Now, the woman waked them earlier still, in the middle of the night, for she could not tell when it was cock-crow.

THE TRAVELING MUSICIANS.

I.

HOW THEY SET OUT.

A FARMER had an Ass that had been a faithful servant to him a great many years; but the Ass was now growing old, and every day was more and more unfit for work.

His master, therefore, was tired of keeping him, and began to think of putting an end to him; but the Ass saw there was mischief in the wind and took himself off slyly; he set out toward the great city. "For there," thought he, "people will like to hear me bray, and I shall earn my living as a musician."

He had traveled a little way when he spied a Dog by the wayside. The Dog was lying down, and panting as if he were very tired.

"What makes you pant so, my friend?" asked the Ass.

"Alas!" said the Dog, "my master was about to knock me on the head. I am old and weak, and can no longer hunt as I used. So I ran away. But how can I earn a living?"

"Hark ye," said the Ass; "I am going to the great city to be a musician; suppose you go with me, and try what you can do in the same way."

" Very well," said the Dog, and they jogged on together.

They had not gone far before they saw a Cat sitting in the middle of the road. The Cat wore a very sad face.

" Pray, my good lady," said the Ass, " what is the matter with you? You look quite out of sorts."

" Ah me ! " said the Cat, " well I may. How can I be in good spirits, when I fear for my life ? I am beginning to grow old, and I like to lie at my ease by the fire, and not to run about the house after mice. So my mistress laid hold of me, and was about to drown me. I was lucky enough to get away from her ; but what am I to live on ? "

" Oh ! " said the Ass, " come with us to the great city. You are a good night singer, and may make your fortune as a musician."

" Well said," said the Cat, and she joined the party.

On they went, until they came to a farm-yard. There they saw a Cock perched upon the gate, and the Cock was crowing with all his might and main.

" Bravo ! " said the Ass ; " upon my word you make a famous noise ; pray, what is all this about ? "

" Why," said the Cock, " I was just now saying that it was going to be fine weather, when lo! the cook claps her hands to her ears, and says she means to cut my head off, and make broth of me for the guests that are coming to-morrow."

"What a shame!" said the Ass. "But come with us, master Cock. It will be better than to stay here and have your head cut off. Besides, who knows? If we take care to sing in tune, we may get up some kind of a concert; so, come along with us."

"With all my heart," said the Cock; and they all four went on their merry way.

II.

HOW THEY GAVE A CONCERT.

THEY could not reach the great city the first day; so, when night came on, they went into the wood to sleep. The Ass and the Dog lay down under a great tree; the Cat climbed up and sat on a branch; the Cock flew up to the top of the tree, for that was a very safe place.

Before he went to sleep, he looked out on all sides to see if the world were quiet. Afar off he saw something bright, and he called out to the others:—

"There must be a house no great way off, for I see a light."

"If that be the case," said the Ass, "let us change our quarters, for our lodging here is not the best in the world."

"So say I," said the Dog. "I should not be the worse for a bone or two, or a bit of meat."

So off they all went to the spot where the Cock had seen the light; as they drew near, it became larger and brighter, till at last they came close to a house in which a gang of robbers lived.

The Ass was the tallest of the company, so he marched up to the window and peeped in.

"Well, Ass," said the Cock, "what do you see?"

"What do I see? Why, I see a table spread with all sorts of good things, and men sitting round it, making merry."

"That would be a fine place for us to live in," said the Cock.

"Yes," said the Ass, "if we only could get in." So they all talked the matter over, and at last hit upon a plan. The Ass stood on his hind-legs, with his fore-feet resting on the window-sill; the Dog got upon his back; the Cat scrambled up to the Dog's shoulders, and the Cock flew up and sat upon the Cat's head.

When all was ready, they began their music. The Ass brayed, the Dog barked, the Cat mewed, and the Cock crowed; and then they all broke through the window at once, and came tumbling into the room; the glass fell with a smash upon the floor, and there was a great clatter.

The robbers started when they heard the music; they were scared out of their wits when the Traveling Musicians came tumbling into the room; and so they took to their heels at once.

III.

HOW THEY MADE THEMSELVES AT HOME.

As soon as they were gone, the Traveling Musicians sat down at the table; they ate all that the robbers had left, and as they were very hungry, they ate very fast.

Then, when they had cleared the table, they put out the lights, and each found a place in which to sleep. The Ass lay upon a heap of straw in the yard; the Dog stretched himself upon a mat behind the door; the Cat rolled herself up on the hearth before the warm ashes; and the Cock perched upon a beam at the top of the house. They were all tired and soon fell asleep.

After some time the robbers, who had not fled far, got over their fright. They saw that the lights were out, and that all was quiet.

They began to think they had been frightened at nothing. One, bolder than the rest, crept back to the house. All was still ; all was dark.

He made his way into the kitchen, and groped about to find a candle. He found the candle, and then went to the fire, as he thought, to light his candle. But the live coals which he thought he saw were the two fiery eyes of the Cat.

He held the candle close, to light it, but the Cat, not liking the joke, sprang at his face, and spit, and scratched him. Away he ran to the door ; but there the Dog jumped up and bit him in the leg ; as he was crossing the yard, the Ass kicked him, and the Cock, now awake, crowed with all his might.

At this, the robber ran back to his comrades, as fast as his legs could carry him. He told them that a horrid witch had got into the house, and had spit at him, and scratched his face with long bony fingers ; that a man with a knife in his hand hid behind the door, and stabbed him in the leg ; that a black monster stood in the yard, and struck him with a club ; and that the judge sat upon the top of the house, and cried out : —

" Throw the rascal up here ! "

After this, the robbers never dared to go back to the house. The Traveling Musicians were so pleased with their quarters, that they took up their abode there, and there they are, I dare say, at this very day.

THE KITE AND THE PIGEONS.

THE Pigeons had long lived in fear of the Kite; but by being always on the look-out, and by keeping close to the pigeon-house, they made out to live in safety.

The Kite found he could not take them boldly; so he tried a trick. He went to the pigeon-house and said: —

"Why do you live all the time in fear of me? I am strong and could keep away all things that might hurt you. Make me your king."

"Well said," thought the Pigeons, and they made the Kite their king. But when the Kite was once inside the pigeon-house, he shut the door; and then he ate the Pigeons, one each day.

"It serves us right," said one of them, when his turn came.

THE CAT AND THE MICE.

THERE was a house which was overrun with Mice. A Cat found this out, and went there and began to catch them. At this, the Mice hid for safety in the eaves, and the Cat saw that

she must catch them by a trick. She climbed
up to the eaves and held by her hind legs to a
peg; there she hung as if she were dead.

One of the Mice peeped out and saw her
there; but he said : —

"Aha, you fellow! If you were a bag of
meal, we would not come out to you."

CLEVER ALICE.

I.

SHE SHOWS HOW PRUDENT SHE IS.

ONCE upon a time there was a man who had
a daughter, who was called Clever Alice. When
she was grown up, her father said : —

"We must see about her marrying."

"Yes," said her mother; "as soon as a
young man shall appear who is worthy of her."

At last, a youth, by name Hans, came from
a town near by, and asked to marry her.

"But," he said, "I cannot marry your daughter unless she is very prudent."

"Oh," said her father; "never fear for that!
she has a head full of brains." And the mother
added : —

"Ah, she can see the wind blow up the
street, and hear the flies cough."

" Very well," said Hans ; " but mind, if she is not very prudent, I will not take her."

Soon they all sat down at dinner, and her mother said : —

"Alice, go down into the cellar and draw some cider."

So Clever Alice took the jug down from the shelf, and went into the cellar. As soon as she was down-stairs, she drew a stool and placed it before the cask, in order that she might not have to stoop ; for she thought stooping might hurt her back.

Then she placed the jug before her, and turned the tap. She did not wish her eyes to be idle, so, while the cider was running, she looked about upon the wall above and below. As she peeped here and peeped there she saw a hatchet, which some workmen had left sticking into a beam right over her head. At sight of this, Clever Alice began to cry, saying : —

"Oh, oh ! if I marry Hans, and we have a child, and he grows up, and we send him into the cellar to draw cider, this hatchet will fall on his head and kill him !" and so she sat there weeping to think of this ill chance.

II.

ALL FIND OUT HOW PRUDENT ALICE IS.

Now the good people up-stairs were waiting for their cider, and as Clever Alice did not come, her mother sent the maid to go and see what was the matter. The maid went down into the cellar, and there was Clever Alice on the stool before the cask, crying heartily.

" Alice," she asked, " what are you weeping about ? "

" Ah ! " said she, " have I not cause ? If I marry Hans, and we have a child, and he grows up, and we send him into the cellar to draw cider, this hatchet will fall on his head and kill him."

" Oh," said the maid, " what a prudent Alice we have ! " and sitting down, she began to weep too, to think of this ill chance.

By and by, when the maid did not come back, the good people up-stairs began to feel very thirsty ; so the husband told the boy to go down into the cellar to see what had become of Alice and the maid. The boy went down, and there sat Clever Alice and the maid, both crying.

" What now ? " he asked, looking at Clever Alice. " What are you crying for ? "

" Ah," said she, " have I not cause ? If I

marry Hans, and we have a child, and he grows up, and we send him into the cellar to draw cider, this hatchet will fall on his head and kill him."

" Oh," said the boy, " what a prudent Alice we have ! " and he fell to weeping with the others.

Up-stairs sat the good people ; they waited and waited, and at last the husband said : —

" Do you go down-stairs, wife, and see what keeps Alice so long."

So she went down, and found all three weeping together.

" What does this mean ? " she asked. " Alice weeping ? the maid weeping ? the boy weeping ? what is the trouble ? "

" Ah," said Alice, " have I not cause ?   If I marry Hans, and we have a child, and he grows up, and we send him into the cellar to draw cider, this hatchet will fall on his head and kill him."

" Oh," said the mother. " What a prudent Alice we have ! " and she sat down and began to weep as much as the others.

Now the husband sat above with Hans, and they waited and waited.   At last he felt so very thirsty that he said : —

" I must go down myself into the cellar, and see what is keeping our Alice."

So down he went, and found Alice, the maid, the boy, and his wife all weeping as if their hearts would break.

" Dear soul!" said he to Clever Alice, " what troubles you ?"

" Ah," said Alice, " have I not cause ? If I marry Hans, and we have a child, and he grows up, and we send him into the cellar to draw cider, this hatchet will fall on his head and kill him."

" Ah," said the father, " what a prudent Alice we have," and he sat down and began to cry with the whole strength of his lungs.

All this time Hans sat alone up-stairs. He waited and waited, but nobody came. So he went down to see what was the matter. There he saw all five in a row, weeping and wailing.

" Good people," said he, " what is going on ? Why do you weep ?" and he turned to the husband.

" Ask my wife," said he.

" Ask the boy," said she.

" Ask the maid," said he.

" Ask Alice," said she. And Alice said : —

" Have I not cause ? If I marry you, and we have a child, and he grows up, and we send him into the cellar to draw cider, this hatchet will fall on his head and kill him. Do you not think this is enough to weep about ?"

"Now," said Hans, "no one could be more prudent than this girl. So, if you will, Clever Alice, I will marry you."

III.

HOW VERY CLEVER SHE PROVED TO BE.

AFTER they had been married a little while, Hans said one morning : —

"Wife, I will go out to work to earn some money. Do you go into the field, and gather some corn and make bread."

"That I will, dear Hans," said she. When he was gone, she cooked some nice porridge to take with her. As she came to the field, she asked herself, —

"What shall I do? Shall I cut the corn first, or eat my porridge? I think I will eat first." Then she ate all that was in her bowl. She looked into it; it was empty.

"Now," she asked herself, "shall I cut the corn or take a nap? I think I will take a nap." So she laid herself down among the corn and went fast to sleep.

By and by Hans came home, but no Alice was there.

"Oh," said he, "what a prudent Alice I have. She works so hard that she does not even come home to eat anything."

Evening came, and still Alice did not come home. Then Hans went out to see how much corn she had cut. And lo! nothing at all, and there lay Alice fast asleep among the corn. Off went Hans and brought a net with bells hanging from it. He threw the net over her head, and went back to the house. Then he shut the door, and fell to working at his bench.

It was quite dark when Clever Alice awoke. As soon as she stood up, the net fell over her hair, and the bells jingled at every step she took. She did not know what to make of it, and began to doubt if she were really Clever Alice, and said to herself, —

" Am I she, or am I not ? "

She could not make up her mind how to answer this question. At last she thought she would go home and ask Hans. He would know. She came to the house, but the door was shut. So she tapped on the window, and asked, —

" Hans, is Alice within ? "

" Yes," said he, " she is."

At that, she quite lost her wits.

" Then I am not Alice ! " she cried, and ran to another house, to ask somebody else. But as soon as the folk within heard the bells in her net jingle, they would not open the door. So she ran straight away from the village, and no one has ever seen her since. That is the end of the story of Clever Alice.

THE WOLF AND THE CRANE.

A Wolf once had a bone stuck in his throat, and offered to pay the Crane well if she would thrust her head down, with its long bill, and draw the bone out.

When she had done this, she asked for her pay. Then the Wolf laughed, and showed his teeth, and said : —

"Is it not enough for you that you have had your head in a Wolf's mouth, and have drawn it out again safely ? What more do you want?"

THE FROGS ASK FOR A KING.

In old times, we read, the Frogs lived in a free and easy way, each one as he pleased. But the elders among them did not like this, and begged Jove to send them a king.

Jove thought them very foolish, and tossed a log into the middle of the pond. The Frogs were scared out of their wits, and plunged at once into the deepest hole. By and by, they peeped out and saw that King Log was stockstill.

They began to grow bolder ; soon they laughed at King Log ; then they jumped up and sat on the log. That was not a king, they said, and off they went to Jove, and asked him to give them a new king.

This time Jove gave them an Eel; but the Eel was stupid, and the Frogs liked him no better. They sent a third time to Jove.

At this Jove was angry, and sent them a king of another sort. For he sent them King Stork, and King Stork caught the Frogs, one by one, and ate them, till there was not one left.

THE GOLDEN BIRD.

I.

THE BIRD CARRIES OFF THE APPLES.

A KING had a fair garden, and in the garden was a tree, and the tree bore apples of gold. Every morning these apples were counted; and every morning there was one apple less. The king grew very angry and bade the gardener keep watch all night under the tree.

The gardener set his eldest son to watch; but about twelve o'clock he fell asleep, and in the morning another apple was gone. Then the second son was told to watch; at twelve o'clock he fell asleep, and in the morning another apple was gone.

Then the third son said he would watch. The gardener would not let him at first, for fear some harm would come to him. But at last he gave him leave, and the young man lay down under the tree to watch.

As the clock struck twelve, he heard a rustling noise in the air, and a bird came flying toward him. The bird was of pure gold, and snapped at one of the apples with his beak. The gardener's son jumped up, and shot an arrow at the bird, but did it no harm. Only a golden feather fell to the ground from its tail, as the bird flew away.

In the morning, the feather was carried to the king. All the wise men were called together, and they said the feather was worth all the wealth of the kingdom. But the king said : —

" One feather is of no use to me; I must have the whole bird."

II.

TWO BROTHERS SET OUT TO FIND THE BIRD.

THEN the gardener's eldest son set out to find the golden bird. He had gone but a little way, when he came to a wood, and by the side of the wood he saw a Fox. So he took his bow and made ready to shoot at it. Then the Fox said : —

" Do not shoot me, for I will give you good counsel. I know what you want; you wish to find the golden bird. You will come to a vil-

lage in the evening. When you get there you
will see two inns over against each other. One
of them is pleasant to look at; go not in there,
but rest for the night in the other, though it
seem to you very poor and mean." But the
eldest son thought to himself : —

"What can such a beast as this know about
the matter?" So he shot his arrow at the Fox,
but he missed aim. The Fox set up its tail over
its back and ran into the wood. Then the eldest
son went his way, and in the evening came to the
village where the two inns were. In one of
them were people singing and dancing and feast-
ing; the other looked poor and mean.

"I should be very silly," he said, "if I went
to that shabby house, and left this pleasant
place." So he went into the smart house, and
ate and drank and took his ease, and forgot the
golden bird and his own home.

Time passed on. As the eldest son came not
back, and no tidings were brought of him, the
second son set out, and the same thing happened
to him. He met the Fox, who gave him the
same advice. But when he came to the two
inns, his elder brother was standing at the window, where the sport was going on, and called
to him to come in. He could not resist, but
went in and forgot the golden bird and his own
home.

III.

THE YOUNGEST SON SEEKS THE GOLDEN BIRD.

TIME passed on again, and the youngest son wished to set out into the wide world to seek the golden bird; but for a long while his father would not hear of it; he was very fond of his son, and was afraid that some ill luck would happen to him also, and prevent him from coming back.

At last he let him go, for the boy would not rest at home. He too went to the wood and met the Fox, and heard the same words. But he thanked the Fox, and did not shoot at him, as his brothers had done.

"Sit upon my tail," said the Fox, "and you will travel faster." So he took his seat on the Fox's tail; the Fox began to run, and away they went over stock and stone, so fast that their hair whistled in the wind.

When they came to the village, the youngest son followed the counsel of the Fox, and went straight into the shabby inn, and rested there all night. In the morning the Fox met him, as he was about to set out, and said : —

"Go straight on, until you come to a castle, with a troop of soldiers fast asleep before the gate. Take no heed of them, but go into the castle, and pass on and on until you come to a room, where the golden bird sits in a wooden cage. Close by it stands a beautiful golden cage; do not try to take the bird out of the shabby cage and put it into the handsome one, or you will surely repent of it." Then the Fox stretched out his tail again, and the youngest son sat on it, and away they went over stock and stone, so fast that their hair whistled in the wind.

IV.

THE BIRD IS FOUND AND LOST.

IT was as the Fox had said. There was the castle, and before it the troop of soldiers fast asleep. The youngest son pushed in and came to the room where the golden bird hung in a wooden cage. Near by stood a golden cage, and the golden apples that had been lost were lying by it. Then he thought to himself : —

"It would be odd to bring away such a fine bird in a shabby cage." So he opened the door, and took hold of the bird to put it into the golden cage. At that the bird set up a scream. All the soldiers awoke and seized the youngest son, and carried him off to the king.

The next morning the court sat in judgment. They heard what he had done, and then they sentenced him to death, unless he should bring

the king the golden horse, which could run as
swiftly as the wind. If he did this, he was to
live, and was to have the golden bird for his
own.

V.

THE GOLDEN HORSE.

So the youngest son set out once more on his
travels. He was in a sad state of mind, when
on a sudden his friend, the Fox, met him, and
said : —

"You see now what happened because you
did not heed my words. But I will tell you
how to find the golden horse, only you must do
as I bid you. You must go straight on till you
come to the castle where the horse stands in his
stall. By his side will lie the groom fast asleep.
Take away the horse quietly, but be sure to put
the old leather saddle upon him, and not the
golden one which is close by."

Then the youngest son sat upon the Fox's tail,
and away they went over stock and stone, so fast
that their hair whistled in the wind.

All went well. There was the golden horse
in his stall, and there lay the groom asleep, with
his hand upon the golden saddle. But when
the youngest son looked at the horse, he thought
it a great pity to put the leather saddle upon
him.

"I will give him the best one," said he ; "I am sure he deserves it." So he took up the golden saddle; but as he did this, the groom awoke and cried aloud; all the guards ran in and made him prisoner, and in the morning he was brought before the court. His doom was to die, but the judges said that he might live if he could bring to the king the beautiful princess ; not only should he live, but he was to have the golden bird and the golden horse for his own.

VI.

THE BEAUTIFUL PRINCESS.

THE youngest son went his way very sad, but the old Fox came to him again, and said : —

" Why did you not listen to me ? If you had listened, you would have carried away both the bird and the horse. But attend. Go straight on, and in the evening you will arrive at a castle. At twelve o'clock at night, the princess will come into the hall. Go up to her, and take her hand, and she will let you lead her away. But take care you do not suffer her to go and take leave of her father and mother." Then the Fox stretched out his tail, and away they went over stock and stone, so fast that their hair whistled in the wind.

They came to the castle, and all was as the Fox had said. At twelve o'clock the youngest son met the princess as she came into the hall. He took her hand, and she agreed to run away with him, but begged with many tears that he would let her take leave of her father and mother.

At first he would not, but she wept still more and more, and fell at his feet, till at last he consented. But the moment she came to her father's house, the guards awoke and took the youngest son prisoner. He was brought before the father of the princess, who said : —

" You shall never have my daughter, unless in eight days you dig away the hill that stops the view from my window."

Now this hill was so big that a thousand men working a thousand days could not take it away; but the youngest son went to work. When he had digged for seven days, the Fox came to him and said : —

" Lie down, and go to sleep. I will work for you."

In the morning the youngest son awoke, and the hill was gone. So he went merrily in, and told the father of the princess that now he must give him his daughter. The father said he would keep his word, and away went the youngest son and the princess.

VII.

THE PRINCESS, THE HORSE, AND THE BIRD.

THEN the Fox came and said : —

" We will have all three, the princess, the horse, and the bird."

" Ah," said the youngest son, " that would be a fine thing ! but how will you bring it about ? "

" If you will only listen, it can soon be done. When you come to the king, and he asks for the beautiful princess, you must say, ' Here she is ! ' Then he will be very joyful, and you will mount the golden horse that they are to give you, and put out your hand to take leave of them ; but shake hands with the princess last. When you take her hand, lift her quickly upon the horse ; seat her behind you, clap your spurs to his side, and gallop away as fast as you can."

All went well. Then the Fox came to him again, and said : —

" When you come to the castle where the bird is, I will stay with the princess at the door ; you will ride in and speak to the king. When he sees that you are on the golden horse he will bring out the bird. But you must sit still and say that you want to look at it, to see if it be the true golden bird. When you get it in your hand, ride away."

This too happened as the Fox had said. They carried off the bird, the princess mounted again, and they rode on to a great wood. Then the Fox came and said : —

" Pray kill me, and cut off my head and my feet."

But the youngest son would not do this. So the Fox said : —

" I will at any rate give you good counsel. Beware of two things. Do not save any one from being hanged, and sit down by no river." Then away he went.

VIII.

HOW THE YOUNGEST SON LOST EVERYTHING.

" WELL," thought the youngest son, " it is no hard matter to keep such advice as that." He rode on with the princess, till at last he came to the village where he had left his two brothers. There he heard a great uproar, and when he asked what was the matter the people said : —

" Two men are to be hanged."

As he came near, he saw that the two men were his brothers, who had turned robbers, so he asked : —

" Cannot they in any way be saved ? "

But the people said, " No," unless he would

give all his money to buy liberty for the rascals. He did not stop to think about the matter, but paid what was asked, and his brothers were given up, and went on with him toward their home.

As they came to the wood where the **Fox** first met them, it was so cool and pleasant that the brothers said : —

" Let us sit down by the side of the river, and rest awhile, to eat and drink." The youngest son forgot the Fox's counsel and said " Yes," and sat down by the side of the river. He was fearing nothing, when the brothers came behind, and threw him down the bank, and took the princess, the horse, and the bird, and went home to the king, their master.

" All this have we won by our labor," they said, and then was there great joy. But the horse would not eat, the bird would not sing, and the princess wept.

IX.

THE YOUNGEST SON COMES TO THE THRONE.

Now the youngest son fell to the bottom of the river. Luckily, it was nearly dry, but he was badly bruised, and the bank was so steep that he could not climb out. Then the Fox

came once more, and scolded him for not following his advice.

"Yet," said he, "I cannot leave you here.
So lay hold of my tail and hold fast." Then
he pulled him out of the river, and said to him,
as he stood upon the bank : —

"Your brothers have set watch to kill you if
they find you in the kingdom."

So he dressed himself as a poor man, and
came in secret to the king's court. Scarcely
was he within the doors when the horse began
to eat, the bird began to sing, and the princess
left off weeping. Then he went to the king
and told him what rogues his brothers had been.
The king seized the brothers and clapped them
into prison. The youngest son got the princess
again, and after the king's death he was heir to
the kingdom.

A long while after, he went to walk one day
in the wood. The Fox, now grown old, met
him, and begged him with tears in his eyes to
kill him, and cut off his head and feet. At last,
being much urged, he did so, and lo ! the Fox
was changed into a man, and turned out to be
the princess's brother, who had been lost a great
many years.

INDEX.

www.ingramcontent.com/pod-product-compliance
Lightning Source LLC
Chambersburg PA
CBHW030541040726
47497CB00008B/2538